18.95 ✔

Hickory Homes
175 W. Hickory
Hesston, KS 67062

TEA WITH MR TIMOTHY

Tea with Mr Timothy

GEOFFREY MORGAN

Illustrated by Nicholas Fisk

ISIS
LARGE PRINT
Oxford, England

First published in Great Britain 1964
by Max Parrish and Co Ltd

Published in Large Print 1992 by Clio Press,
55 St. Thomas' Street, Oxford OX1 1JG,
by arrangement with Chapmans Publishers Ltd

British Library Cataloguing in Publication Data
Morgan, Geoffrey
Tea with Mr Timothy. — New ed
I. Title
823.914 [F]

ISBN 1-85695-300-9

Printed and bound by Hartnolls Ltd, Bodmin, Cornwall
Cover designed by CGS Studios Ltd, Cheltenham

For Betty

PROLOGUE

They say the cat has nine lives. Perhaps some cats have. Mr Timothy had only one, but he would not have exchanged it with any cat in the neighbourhood who had the other eight.

No one would blame him for that, for he was the fortunate recipient of a great affection; watched over, waited upon, and sheltered from the ugly world outside the windows of the house in Angel Street. His proud indifference was forgiven, his occasional lapse of temper overlooked; his every whim granted. Only his intense curiosity in the life outside was never satisfied. Then one afternoon in November, Guy Fawkes' day of all days, he slipped out . . . And thus began his story.

But this is not wholly Mr Timothy's story. It belongs also to the three people whose life he shared and influenced during those short, carefree years between the Mid-Thirties and the Flaming Era of Violence that followed within the decade.

CHAPTER
ONE

If you ever passed through Angel Street in those early days you must have noticed Miss Pilgrim's house. It stood back from the dingy row of properties flanking one side of the road. Its paintwork was shabby and faded, brick and mortar grimed with soot from the railway embankment opposite, yet it still retained a prim, dignified appearance. If you had seen Miss Pilgrim you might have described her in something of the same way, too. Frail, elderly; a picture of lavender and faded lace, yet noble of figure and touching in her simple dignity.

But should you by chance have overlooked Miss Pilgrim or the house, you could not have failed to notice her cat. Mr Timothy always sat in the window to the right of the front door, a great black and white figure of fur, framed between the white lace curtains like some eminent star acknowledging his public's applause. Everyone noticed

1

him who passed through Angel Street. Everyone, that is, but Ginger.

Ginger only went that way when he was in a hurry. It was a short cut to Lacey Market. He usually ran through the street because he was late, and on such occasions he would have noticed nothing, for his young mind was fully occupied with the excuses he was going to make to Mr Massey. If there ever was a time when his attention was not so engaged and he might have had eyes for the cat in the window, Mr Timothy was probably in the parlour having tea. Thus it was when Ginger saw the cat for the first time Mr Timothy was not the sedate figure in the window. He was a frantic, terrified animal crouching in the arms of a little girl, and it was Guy Fawkes' day.

Ginger was an orphan. He had a round cheerful face that made his figure look so thin, and a mop of unruly hair that was more chestnut in colour than carrot. In his long baggy trousers and patched jersey he presented an urchin appearance that defied any accuracy in guessing his age, though he would have proudly told you himself he was rising fourteen. Almost any time of the day, and anywhere between Commercial Road and Mile End, you might have seen him pushing Mr Massey's junk barrow through the East End streets.

But on this particular November afternoon the barrow contained something more exciting than the odds and ends that went to make up Mr Massey's stock-in-trade; it contained a guy, fashioned by Ginger's patient hands from the sacking, cardboard and straw he had raked out of the garbage shed behind the junk shop. A pair of Ginger's ragged trousers covered the stumpy legs. The old jacket and hat he had pilfered from the rag cupboard to which Mr Massey consigned the secondhand clothes he couldn't sell, and a brightly-coloured mask Ginger had bought for a penny completed the image.

He was proud of his creation, knew it to be the best in the district, and his feeling of achievement was only occasionally marred when he thought about the barrow. For the barrow belonged to Mr Massey, and he had taken it without permission. The thought pricked at his conscience, for Mr Massey was, on the whole, a kindly man (except when he had one of his coughing fits) and Ginger had never — well, almost never — deceived or disobeyed him ever since the little junk man had taken him under his wing so many years before. Ginger knew no other father — or mother. Mr Massey had been both and when he reached his teens the man became his employer also. Ginger still attended school — when Mr Massey had no special job for him — and in-between-times, there were always errands to run, the shop to sweep out, and the barrow to push somewhere to collect or deliver the odd assortment of goods Mr Massey bought and sold.

He was thinking about the barrow when he crossed the top of Angel Street, so the wild cries and laughter wafted to him in a pall of smoke from the engine on the embankment did not at first attract his attention. He was on his way to the station in the hope of adding to the three coppers in the battered cocoa tin displayed suggestively at the guy's feet, and he was wondering whether he could increase these meagre earnings at the station and get back to the shop in Button Row before Mr Massey returned and discovered he had taken the barrow. Mr Massey had shut the shop for the afternoon and had gone to visit his sick sister in Leytonstone, an event that occurred at infrequent intervals, but Ginger could never be sure whether these excursions would bring the old man back in time for tea or supper. Three coppers would buy few fireworks, but if he was caught out with the barrow Ginger wouldn't get any fireworks at all. And already the afternoon was fading and street lamps were glimmering through the smoky twilight.

He had reached the gutter on the opposite side when the sounds from Angel Street finally registered, and he paused, staring down the grimy road towards the railway arches at the end. At first he thought the faint squealing came from the embankment and was the sound of brakes on shunting goods wagons; then he heard the loud derisive laughter of boys, and the faint cry of a girl, then the squeal again, like a stifled shriek of helplessness and terror. He heard a firework explode and thought it was a Ha'penny Demon or a Thunderbolt. Even in the noise of the shuffling engine along the embankment, the explosion was loud, its echo thrown back and forth between the railway arches and the houses opposite.

Ginger hesitated no longer, but ran down the street, pushing the barrow ahead of him. Half-way down he could see quite clearly the small group of boys dancing and gesticulating around a little girl who was protecting something in her arms. It didn't take Ginger many seconds to understand the situation, and as soon as he realised the girl was clutching a cat, he knew the gang of ruffians were attempting to hitch a firework to its tail.

Ginger loved all animals, and especially soft, furry creatures, and his feeling for them was strengthened by Mr Massey's refusal to have a pet in the place. This denial was the one great pang in Ginger's life, and many a night as he lay in bed in the little box room over the kitchen he shivered with apprehension when he heard the rattle of the dustbin lid or clatter of garbage cans in the back yard, for almost at once came the sound of Mr Massey's window jerking open, an angry oath, and then the splash of water as the china jug was emptied into the yard. Ginger didn't mind the water so much; it couldn't harm the cats. It was when some more solid object was thrown that he prayed for the safety of the stray prowlers. There was nothing else he could do about it. Mr Massey only disliked dogs. But he hated cats. He called them messy scavengers. So although Ginger was sure many of the cats he saw when going about his errands were homeless orphans, he never dare give one of them encouragement for fear it followed him to the shop.

But he had never seen this cat before. Nor the girl. Neither did he know the boys grouped around her except for one skinny, pimply-faced urchin whom he thought he recognised from Lacey Market. There were five of them altogether, led by a fat bully in long trousers who was waving a firework in his hand. Ginger was so incensed by the scene that he didn't stop to consider either his own safety or the danger to his guy and barrow, but lunged forward into the group, using the vehicle like a tank.

The front of the barrow hit the fat boy squarely across the buttocks and threw him violently forward and he collided with two of his companions. They fell back against the wall, and slithered to the ground. The other two youngsters retreated so that the circle around the girl was broken, and she ran across the road, her terrified burden almost leaping from her arms. The firework which the fat boy had dropped suddenly exploded and Ginger withdrew through the thin smoke-screen, but the pimply-faced one had recognised him.

"It's Ginger!" he shouted, pointing an accusing finger for the benefit of his leader. "Arter 'im!"

The fat boy was on his feet, and sweeping his arm in a raging gesture of encouragement, rushed at Ginger followed by his shrieking, bloodthirsty gang.

Ginger backed away, unable to defend himself without leaving go of the barrow which he knew would be smashed if he left it, and in the mêlée of arms, legs and bloodcurdling shrieks surrounding him in the next moment he was painfully aware of the gap in his defences. The vicious swing of the fat boy's fist caught Ginger on the side of the mouth and he staggered backwards across the road, but still grasping the shafts of the barrow which, like the guy, was now kicked and pummelled by the younger hoodlums.

Ginger retreated slowly but defiantly, and in an agonising daze he was conscious of many things — the warm, salty taste of blood in his mouth, the glazed, triumphant look of the fat boy as he came at him again with flailing arms, the rattle of the cocoa tin on the cobbles, the unrecognisable heap that had once been his guy; but most of all he was conscious of the cries of shame and alarm the girl with the cat shouted at his attackers. She was somewhere just behind him.

It was the approach of a man through the arch that broke up the fight, and the gang scattered in all directions and vanished from the street. The scene was calm again. Even the grinding discord of shunting wagons receded along the embankment so that Ginger heard the ominous scraping and lumbering of the wheels struggling to turn as he pulled the barrow into the gutter. The man whose arrival had quashed the disturbance passed by the end of Angel Street, unconscious of the incident that had taken place a few yards from the arches and the effect his coming had upon it.

Ginger stood dejectedly in the gutter, his eyes smarting and lips throbbing, as he surveyed the broken barrow and the ugly mess of straw and tattered clothing. Some of the wooden spokes in the wheels were cracked or broken, one side was stove in, the thin strakes forming the front rail were smashed. It had never been a very good barrow; but that was no consolation. He stared at the wreckage in miserable silence, hardly aware of the company when the girl sidled shyly up to him.

"I'm sorry — Ginger," she said in a small voice, but he might not have heard her; he was wondering how Mr Massey would take it.

"Thank you for — for — rescuing us," she tried again. "You're brave. If you hadn't come those dreadful bullies would have killed Mr Timothy."

Ginger dragged his eyes from the barrow and stared at her curiously.

"Mister Timothy?" he repeated.

The girl nodded and buried her chin in the long black fur of the cat hugged in her arms.

"This is Mr Timothy," she said.

"Mr Timothy," he muttered, gently stroking the soft fur. "That's a funny sort of a name for a cat."

The object of their attention settled more comfortably in the fold of her arms. He began to purr. It was a strong, husky sound that seemed to start somewhere deep inside the huge body. Ginger could feel the vibrations under his hand as he stroked the cat's back.

He spoke to the cat and for a moment forgot everything

7

else. But Mr Timothy was quite indifferent now. He gazed at Ginger through half-closed eyes completely unappreciative of what the boy had done for him. Ginger was looking at the face. It was a nice face, round and furry with the longest whiskers he had ever seen. The ears stood up sharp, and were very clean. The black nose shone so, it might have been polished. Around his mouth the fur changed abruptly from black to white and this streaked under his chin and down his chest in a heart-shaped contour to end in almost a point between his front legs. It looked like a bib just out of the wash-tub. Except for this and the white smudges on the tops of each paw his coat was a glossy black.

"He's a fine fella," muttered Ginger. "But it's a funny sort of a name."

"It's my aunt's name," said the girl.

Ginger glanced up at her, more curious than ever.

The girl smiled and dimples peeped in her cheeks.

"What I mean is — well, Aunt Ann gave him the name. She's always called him Mister because he's such a gentleman. You see," she leaned towards him confidentially, "she never had a real Mister of her own."

Ginger couldn't quite see how that explained it; but he was too worried to ask any more questions. He stopped stroking the cat and walked round the barrow trying to assess how much damage had been done.

"Your mouth's bleeding," the girl said suddenly, following him round the barrow and anxiously peering at the bruised place. She had wide violet eyes and in the frame of her dark hair her face looked paler than it really was. "You'd better come to the house and wash it."

Ginger wiped the back of his hand across his lips and sniffed. Then looked at the dab of blood on his fingers.

"It's nothink much," he said. "The barrer's a lot worse. And it's not mine."

"Oh dear," said the girl in alarm. "Will you get into trouble?"

"Not much!" he scoffed. "Mr Massey don't take no excuses."

"Oh, dear!" she repeated.

"What's more, he don't know I got it."

"Oh." It was a very sympathetic sound, the way she said it. "That makes it much worse."

"Much worse," he agreed.

"Well, we must do *something*," she said, and then suddenly pointed to the heap in the barrow. "What was that?"

"Just a guy. Made it this morning." He sniffed again. "They done a proper job on it *and* pinched the tin."

"Tin?"

"Tin I had the money in."

"How much have you lost?"

"Only thru'pence in money." Ginger stared at the barrow and wondered how many thru'pences it would take to repair it. He wondered how many months it would take him to pay Mr Massey from his casual earnings. He stopped counting after six. He couldn't see the future after that.

"We shall have to tell Aunt Ann," the girl was saying. "She'll help you. I know she will when she hears what you've done. Besides, you must bathe your lip." She snuggled the cat to her breast and started to walk up the street.

Because Ginger didn't know what else to do, he followed her, trundling the barrow in jerky movements behind him.

CHAPTER
TWO

Ginger managed to get the barrow through the gateway of the house to which the girl led him. He was afraid to leave it in the street lest the gang should return and complete the job they had so ably begun. He closed the gate and stood with the girl as she knocked on the front door, nervously looking around him.

"Now, listen, Ginger," she whispered. "Let *me* tell my aunt how it happened. Don't you say anything till you're asked."

"All right," he said. "But how did you know my name?"

"One of those bullies shouted it."

"Well, what's yours?"

"Jo — and my aunt is Miss Pilgrim," she added.

Ginger nodded and looked vaguely at the cat. What was in a name? Still, it did seem puzzling to call a cat Mister, and a girl by a boy's name, and wasn't that book Larry Fisher got as a prize for going to Sunday School something to do with a pilgrim? It was all a bit of a mix-up coming, as it did, on top of the violent events of the afternoon.

The door opened and a lady stood there. Ginger knew she was a fine lady. The sort of lady he thought his mother might have been. She wore a nice crinkly dress, and although she was thin and her hair almost grey there was a kindly sort of look about her that made the chill November afternoon seem warm. Even now, when the expression on her pale face turned from surprise to something like alarm and distress he had the feeling that everything was going to be all right.

"Josephine, dear child!" she exclaimed. "Whatever's happened?"

Miss Pilgrim didn't appear to notice Ginger. He hung back further and let Jo and Mr Timothy have the limelight. He watched her reach down and gently lift the cat into her arms, fondling his head just as he'd seen Mrs Abrahams do. Only she did it to her baby.

"How could he have got out? Where did you find him?"

Jo began to explain. She had come back from the Corner Stores with some candy bars, and had seen a cat outside the gate. She didn't dream it was Mr Timothy — until she was close to him — and when she went to pick him up he ran off down the street. She caught him under the railway arches. There, a gang of boys had suddenly surrounded her and tried to snatch him. They were going to fix a firework to his tail. She was very afraid, and so was Mr Timothy. She thought he would go out of his mind.

Jo paused breathless. Her story had flowed out so quickly.

As she took a deep gulp of air Miss Pilgrim glanced at Ginger.

"Who is this then?" she asked gently.

"Ginger," Jo said. "He rescued us."

Ginger looked shyly at the lady.

"Hallo," he said.

"He *was so* brave, Aunt Ann," Jo hurried on. "He charged right into the bullies and properly broke them up and Mr Timothy and me got away." She glanced quickly at Ginger. "They smashed up his guy and stole his money tin and nearly wrecked his barrow."

"Mr Massey's barrer," he said quietly.

"And you can see what they did to his face," she said angrily, pointing a finger at his mouth.

Ginger shuffled his feet and stared down at the flagstone path.

"It's nothink," he muttered. "The barrer's worse."

Miss Pilgrim's gaze ranged over his tousled head to the ugly contraption on wheels disfiguring her little square of front garden.

"This is shocking," she said, but her voice was gentle and sympathetic. "Come along in, both of you. We'll see what's to be done."

Ginger was very impressed when he got inside. He'd never seen such luxury before. The room was large and the window had proper curtains over it. There was a carpet on the floor and chairs with soft seats and a long couch with coloured cushions. There were pretty pictures on the walls, and the wall paper was smooth and had a sheen on it fresh as the shiny black grate. The fire burned with little darts of flame and a wisp of steam rose from the spout of the kettle on the hob. In front of the brass-topped fender was a curly rug and at one end a large wicker-basket with a flat cushion in it.

Miss Pilgrim carefully lowered Mr Timothy on to this. He stretched out lazily and then settled down with a white-spatted front paw over the edge of the basket. He yawned at the fire and then gazed up at his mistress as she leaned over, murmuring to him in a strange language. Ginger couldn't understand what she said; neither could anyone else, he was sure. But he supposed Mr Timothy could understand.

Miss Pilgrim took Ginger into the bathroom and lit the geyser. She drew a jug of hot water and filled a china bowl. Then in almost one operation she bathed his mouth and washed the rest of his face. She dabbed some strong-smelling antiseptic on his swollen lip and when he jumped she apologised for the sting, reassuring him that it was not a bad place and would soon heal. Before she left she splashed some more warm water in the bowl and hinted that she liked clean hands at the tea-table.

Ginger gave his hands the best wash they had had for a long time, and while they were soaking in the bowl he studied the copper-coloured geyser. It was a big one with a curving spout over the long, enamelled bath. Low down on one side it had two thin horizontal taps. They moved through a vent in the outer casing, and just beyond them he could see the grids with the holes for the gas jets in them. He wished Mr Massey had got a geyser. It was so much more interesting than the large blackened kettles and the broken-down copper in the scullery behind the shop in Button Row.

His gaze wandered slowly round. Everything glistened white and clean. Even the lavatory was disguised. It had a large wooden top that completely covered the pan and the seat so that at first glance you might take it for a large bathroom stool. There was a cabinet on the wall with a small looking-glass in the door, and over the cane-seated chair was a clean towel which Miss Pilgrim had put there for his use.

He dried his hands and didn't know whether to empty the bowl in the bath or the lavatory. He didn't want to take liberties so he left the water in it. He thought Miss Pilgrim had a reason for leaving the brush and comb in view so he tried to make a parting in his thick, untidy hair. He managed some resemblance to neatness, smoothed down his jersey, and then in the glass watched his finger cautiously explore his swollen lip. It wasn't as bad as it felt. He could hardly see the swelling. He moved back to the door, glancing round once more. Although he knew too much washing made a sissy of you, he liked the bathroom. But he liked the geyser best.

When he returned to the room the table was set for tea. There was a white cloth and a small bowl of pink and white flowers in the centre. There were plates and cups in saucers. Currant bread and a glass dish with a fat slab of butter in it, and strawberry jam and Dundee cake, and next to the teapot on the tray was a jug full of rich cow's milk. Jo knelt on the rug with a toasting fork and beside her was a plate of muffins done crispy brown. Mr Timothy's basket was empty. Ginger could hear his plaintive mewing and Miss Pilgrim's gently coercive voice. He thought they must be in the kitchen.

He stood there, his hands tightly clasped behind him, staring at the table. His mouth would have watered if it hadn't been for the taste of the antiseptic.

Shaking her head to dismiss the dark, wayward curl over her eye, Jo added the last toasted muffin to the heap on the plate and stood up. Ginger moved across quickly and picked up the plate and put it on the table, and she began to spread thick daubs of butter over the muffins.

When Miss Pilgrim came in she was accompanied by an eager Mr Timothy trotting anxiously at her feet, head and tail in the air, wide green-flecked eyes on the saucers his mistress held in each hand. Miss Pilgrim put these on the table and Ginger noticed that one was empty and the other contained a choice piece of fish all nicely cut up into the tiniest portions. It looked like the best part of the inside of a bloater to him. And it had been specially cooked; a faint veil of steam was still rising from it.

Ginger watched Miss Pilgrim spread a large serviette over a portion of the cloth nearest the tray. She put the saucer of fish on this. Then she went to the window and took the potted fern off its high stool and brought the stool back to the table, placing it in front of the saucer. Without any signal from her Mr Timothy suddenly crouched back and sprang on to it. He sat down gently, his eyes on the fish and his tail wrapped round his front paws with its tip sticking up. He sat very still.

Miss Pilgrim invited Ginger to sit down and Jo took her seat at the end of the table. Her aunt sat opposite her and began pouring the tea. Jo passed the muffins to Ginger, and this seemed to be the signal Mr Timothy was waiting for. He suddenly leaned over and began eating the fish.

Ginger couldn't take his eyes off him. He'd never seen a cat with such good manners, and with such understanding ways. He thought he must be a special kind of cat to sit at a table for his tea. It reminded him of a picture he had seen of a circus where two chimpanzees sat down to eat; but they finished up by smacking each other over the head with the teapot and milk jug. Of course, Mr Timothy was much nicer to look at than a chimpanzee; much better behaved. But somehow he seemed just as funny. He looked a bit like an elderly gentleman leaning over his plate afraid he'd spill food down his white bib. He didn't make any noise while he was eating either, unless it was drowned in the crunchy noise Ginger was making as he sank his teeth into his third muffin.

Jo saw him watching the cat and she smiled.

She said: "Mr Timothy always has a high tea."

"He doesn't eat anything midday," explained Miss Pilgrim, as if she were talking about a human being.

Ginger nodded and quickly swallowed the last of the muffin.

"He's got very big on it," he said.

"He's not fully grown up yet, either," Jo said.

"Does he like to sit at the table best?" Ginger asked.

"Yes, he always has," Miss Pilgrim smiled. "He just seemed to understand the way I wanted things right from the beginning. Most of the time I'm on my own. He's my only companion. Why should I have my meals alone when I've such a little gentleman in the house?" She moved her finger affectionately across Mr Timothy's head; but he took no notice. He was indifferent to the conversation. He just went on eating until he had licked the saucer clean.

Miss Pilgrim withdrew it and placed the other saucer before him after pouring out a dash of milk. Mr Timothy licked his chops and, without even a glance around, started to lap.

Ginger was the last to finish. He'd eaten as much as

16

he could before the teapot and milk jug were empty; but he still had room for a third slice of Dundee cake. Miss Pilgrim urged him to have some more, or another piece of currant bread, but stammering his thanks he forced himself to refuse. He thought it would look so bad if he went on eating, especially as Mr Timothy had finished ages ago and was now sitting in his basket washing himself.

Miss Pilgrim was watching him wash with affectionate approval.

"It's a relief to know his wild adventure didn't put him off his food," she said softly, as if talking to herself. "It was a terrible experience." She glanced up suddenly and looked at the boy and the girl. "A terrible experience for you all. I just can't think how he got out of the house."

"It must have been my fault, Aunt Ann," Jo said lamely. "He must have skipped out when I went. I had a job to close the front door. Sometimes it sticks so."

"I know, child," Miss Pilgrim nodded. "I must get Mr Eccles to attend to it."

"I'd never have gone to the stores if I'd known he was out," continued Jo ruefully. "And I lost the candy bars somewhere."

"Never mind, dear," Miss Pilgrim said. "And you're no more to blame than I am."

"Don't Mr Timothy ever go out then, on purpose?" Ginger asked wondrously.

"Not in the streets," said Miss Pilgrim in a firm voice. "It's too dangerous. It wouldn't do for him to mix with other cats. So many of the poor creatures are either diseased, or maimed by fighting. He'd soon come to harm. If he wasn't run over up on the railway there's the same chance in the streets. And if he did avoid disease or disfigurement he would quickly lose condition."

"He's a real house cat," added Jo. "And as proud as a peacock."

Ginger had to agree that he was.

"Of course he has a little run in the back garden," went on Miss Pilgrim. "Mr Eccles made it. He goes out there each day for exercise."

"But he's not really keen on exercise," Jo said. "I was surprised to see him run so fast down the street."

Ginger gazed at Mr Timothy with admiration and curiosity. He certainly lived an unusual life. There was something rather special about him that made him so different from all the other cats. But that might be because he didn't mix with other cats. There was something unusual about Miss Pilgrim, too. But it was a nice unusualness.

"I dread to think what would have happened to my niece and my cat if you hadn't stopped those wicked boys." Miss Pilgrim was looking at Ginger and he could feel the warmth and affection in her grey eyes, but because he had had so little of either, he failed to recognise them for what they were. "I mean to see you right, young man, but first of all you must tell me a few things." She smiled at him. "Where do you live?"

"Button Row," said Ginger. "You just turn off Lacey Market."

"And who's this gentleman — this Mr Massey you mentioned when you spoke about the barrow?"

"He's who I lives with. In the shop in Button Row. It's his barrer. He doesn't know I took it."

Jo suddenly leaned forward over the table.

"Haven't you got — anyone else?"

Ginger shook his head.

Miss Pilgrim looked up from the tablecloth. She put a lace handkerchief up to her mouth and wiped her lips; but she was really clearing her throat.

"Now," she said, quite businesslike. "You live with Mr Massey and he's got a shop and you've got his barrow which is now badly damaged all because of Mr Timothy. Well, we'll take the barrow along to Mr Eccles and get him to repair it. That's the first thing. Then we'll have to explain what happened to Mr Massey." She pressed her fingers to her chin. "There's just one little difficulty. He doesn't know you've got the barrow. How did that come about?"

Ginger thought he'd better explain about that and — well, everything.

In hesitant phrases he told her about Mr Massey and what he bought and sold and how he'd invited Ginger to make his home at the shop. Ginger did his best to repay the kindness and out of school he helped Mr Massey with his business as much as he could. Occasionally Mr Massey gave him some coppers for sweets. For the past few weeks he'd been saving for Guy Fawkes' day, and then the day before yesterday he'd torn his trousers on an old bedstead in the back yard and they were too far gone to mend. Mr Massey had insisted he put his savings towards a new pair, and so he'd given the money back. He knew Mr Massey couldn't afford to buy new trousers or fireworks simply because they might be necessary; but Ginger, having now got the trousers, decided to try and do something about the fireworks. So he'd made a guy that morning and as soon as Mr Massey had closed the shop and gone to Leytonstone, he put the guy in the barrow and started on his rounds.

19

He wasn't worried about losing his guy, he was glad he'd been in time to save Mr Timothy; but he was very worried indeed about the barrow.

Miss Pilgrim didn't say anything, but she seemed to be thinking a lot. He wondered if she was going to tick him off for taking the barrow in the first place. Perhaps she thought his conscience had done that. Jo looked very sad.

"You expect Mr Massey to be angry?" she said.

"He's sure to be," confirmed Ginger. "Specially if he's got one of his coughing fits."

"Does he often get them?" asked Jo.

"Not often. But when he finds out I took the barrer it might give him one and then it'll be worse."

"You mustn't worry." Miss Pilgrim smiled at him again, and her sudden brisk manner suggested that she had a remedy for the trouble. Ginger thought she was the kind of lady who had remedies for everything. "The barrow will be taken care of, and I'll take care of Mr Massey." She stood up, still smiling at Ginger. "We'll take the barrow to Mr Eccles first and then I'll come with you to the shop."

Ginger thanked her and stood up, too. He went over to Mr Timothy and began stroking him while Miss Pilgrim fetched her hat and coat. She asked Jo to clear away the tea things and keep an eye on Mr Timothy while she was gone, and then moved to the door, collecting her handbag on the way. With a final farewell to the now dozy creature in the basket, Ginger joined Miss Pilgrim, and Jo came close and shyly held out her hand. Ginger, just as shyly, grasped it and said good-bye.

"And thank you for rescuing us," Jo added. "I do hope Mr Massey won't be too upset."

Miss Pilgrim made a clucking sound.

20

"Of course he won't when I've explained," she said, smiling. "And what's all this leave-taking? It's surely not the last time we're going to meet you, is it?"

Ginger looked up at her hopefully.

"I trust you'll come and have tea with the three of us again," she suggested.

"When?" Jo asked.

Miss Pilgrim considered. Ginger didn't know what to say.

"Well," said Miss Pilgrim finally. "What about Sunday? Would you like that?"

"Yes," said Ginger. "I'd like that."

CHAPTER
THREE

It was very dark outside except where the street lamps threw a yellowish pool of light around their base. The air was filled with a pungent haze and the sound of exploding fireworks. There were few people in the streets and little traffic so the trundling journey over the worn cobblestones with the barrow to Mr Eccles's yard wasn't as slow and difficult as Ginger had expected.

The joiner's yard was only two streets from Angel Street. You turned right by the railway arches and walked a little way down Colman Row as if you were going to Lacey Market, and then you turned left. Half-way along, where the railway bridge crossed the road, was the entrance to

Mr Eccles's yard. Just inside the double-doors, which were almost under the bridge, was a concrete space where the trucks and barrows loaded and unloaded, and on one side of this, stacked against the wall, were long and short planks of timber, ladders and scaffolding. There was a heap of sand and a bag of cement at the end and to the right of the loading space was the joiner's shop.

It was nothing like a shop really, not such as you'd see in the street. It was more like a small factory. There were long wooden benches, and a small gas engine at one end. This drove wheels with leather belts on that worked the saw and the plane and a thin revolving tool that bored square holes. At the opposite end was an untidy office, and a huge brick fireplace where Mr Eccles heated the glue and boiled the kettle for tea. Everywhere was thick with dust. The windows overlooking the yard were grimed with it, and it lay on the floor like a soft carpet patterned with wood shavings. When the engine was started and the belts whirling, the whole building seemed to tremble with noise, which was only drowned when a train rumbled over the bridge.

Mr Eccles was a little man in a long white apron and a walrus moustache. Having worked under the bridge since he was a boy he was used to the thunder from above and the din around him, and if the dust got into his moustache it never looked dirty. He usually wore a bowler hat with a brim bent and threadbare with age. But he was a clever joiner and could do anything with wood. He lavished the same care and took the same pride in the making of a window sash or a lavatory seat as for a pair of ornamental gates, like the ones he'd just erected for the brewery. He also had a dog who lived on the premises. A little brown and white mongrel Mr Eccles called Jemmy. He was a lithe, hungry-faced little creature who worked for his living by keeping down the rats and mice who made their homes in the sawdust and shavings.

Mr Eccles was mild and always polite and looked the sort of man who was fond of animals. Whenever Ginger had to visit the yard for Mr Massey he always told himself that he would ask Mr Eccles for a job when he left school for good.

Mr Eccles was very polite to Miss Pilgrim. He kept touching his hat respectfully whenever she made a remark as he moved round and round the barrow estimating the damage. In the end he explained that it would be quite a straightforward job; a few new spokes in the wheels, a new rail at the front and another board to replace the broken one in the side. It was pretty sound otherwise. He could get it ready by the next afternoon. Miss Pilgrim agreed the deal and Ginger, feeling a little less anxious, led her silently towards Lacey Market.

Here in the market the business of finding bargains and making profits continued in the light of the hissing naphtha lamps over the stalls, and no one gave a thought to Guy Fawkes or fireworks. The stalls flanked either side of the street, tiny islands of light and noise strung together by shoving people with paper carriers and straw bags. The rows of houses and small shops separated from the stalls by no more than the crowded pavement appeared dead in comparison.

Ginger led Miss Pilgrim along the middle of the street past the vendors of jellied eels and peanuts and fruit till he came to the leather and bootlace stall. Here there was a gap in the traders' line which opened into Button Row.

The street was drab and narrow and the high wall of the button factory fifty yards away brought it to a dead end.

Mr Massey's shop was three doors down, the only shop in the terrace of houses. Its one ground-floor window was little bigger than those of its neighbours and the darkness hid the strange assortment of goods jumbled behind it. One step down was the glass panelled door with strings of coloured beads dangling behind the glass and one or two old magazines with lurid covers clipped to a bit of wire stretched the width of the panel.

There was a light at the back of the shop and Ginger hesitated before knocking. He glanced at Miss Pilgrim but she was looking into her bag. She suddenly pressed a silver shilling into his damp palm and smiled.

"A little something to make up for what you've lost," she said, and thrilled though he was to have a whole shilling to himself, he also realised it was a solid gesture of Miss Pilgrim's support in the coming interview. He knocked boldly on the door.

The white glow at the back of the shop spread to the window, and a moment later they heard a rasping cough. There was a moment's silence, then the light in the shop came on and footsteps approached the door.

"It would be best if you didn't say anythink about Mr Timothy," Ginger whispered desperately. "Mr Massey — er — isn't one for animals."

Miss Pilgrim seemed very cool and collected. Kind and placid though she was, she was not given to easy defeat in matters of principle. She could be very firm and authoritative when occasion demanded; almost like a school teacher, Ginger thought, watching her.

"You introduce me," she said. "And then leave Mr

Massey and me to talk. We'll settle any differences in the matter between ourselves."

As soon as he opened the door and the draught came in Mr Massey began another bout of coughing which he managed to smother with his handkerchief. He apologised for this when he realised that Ginger had a lady with him. He invited them in and hurriedly closed the door.

Ginger glanced shyly at his guardian, uncertain of his mood in spite of the coughing fit. Usually it wasn't easy to tell Mr Massey's feelings from his appearance. His face changed little whatever his mood. It had always been thin and drawn with a lot of lines in it. But the blue eyes were clear and burned with steady penetration. He was short and wiry with a tuft of grey hair and large work-scaled hands. His mouth twitched nervously but eventually it smiled.

"This is Miss Pilgrim, Mr Massey, from Angel Street," Ginger heard himself say quietly.

"At your service, m'lady." Mr Massey inclined his head a fraction as if the movement was a bow.

"I'm pleased to make your acquaintance, Mr Massey," Miss Pilgrim said. "I especially wished to meet you because I wanted you to know of the unselfish action taken by your ward this afternoon on behalf of my little niece and my cat."

Mr Massey blinked just like he might be dazzled, but whether by Miss Pilgrim's gentle and dainty appearance or the forceful yet gracious way she expressed herself, Ginger didn't know. But he thought he'd better take advantage of it while he could.

"I was out with the barrer," he said in a small voice. "And — and there was a — an — accident."

Mr Massey cleared his throat as if he was going to say

something, but instead he started to cough again. Ginger appealed to Miss Pilgrim who nodded her head.

"Mr Massey and I had better sit down and have a quiet talk," she smiled. "I'm sure you won't interrupt us."

"O' course not," said Ginger. "I'll get a chair." He ran into the back room and returned with two bentwood chairs after first making sure they were safe to sit on. He placed them opposite each other in the shop and retreated quickly to the door again.

"Good night, ma'am," he said.

"Good night, young man. And don't forget — tea on Sunday."

Ginger said he'd surely not be forgetting that, and then climbed the stairs to his bedroom before Mr Massey could protest.

But he didn't go to bed for a long time. He stood at the window watching the firework display on a bit of waste ground the other side of the canal. A bonfire was burning and small, dark figures danced around it waving Sparklers and Golden Rains and coloured Roman Candles. The distant flames threw a warm glow into his room and lit up the cracks in the ceiling. But although Ginger's eyes were on the bonfire his mind was downstairs in the shop. Several times he silently opened the door and tip-toed across the bare landing to listen at the top of the stairs. Each time he heard the murmur of conversation. First it was Miss Pilgrim's voice, then he'd recognise the nasal tones of Mr Massey, then Miss Pilgrim again. He thought she must be doing most of the talking which would leave Mr Massey plenty of time for a coughing fit if he was feeling upset. But Ginger never heard him cough at all.

He had no way of knowing what time it was when he

finally heard Mr Massey moving about in the kitchen below, and he guessed that Miss Pilgrim had gone. Outside, it was quiet now. The waste ground was deserted and only the red embers glowed where the bonfire had been. Ginger undressed and put on his flannel nightshirt. He slid into bed as the stairs creaked and quickly buried his head in the covers, feigning sleep.

The door opened gently and after a pause closed again, and he heard Mr Massey in his own room. Ginger uncovered his head and opened his eyes. If Mr Massey had been angry or upset he would have surely spoken or pulled the bedclothes back. Miss Pilgrim must have put everything right.

Soon the next room was silent, but Ginger remained awake, his mind reliving the events of the afternoon. When he did begin to go to sleep he was immediately alerted again by the rattle of the dustbin lid and clatter of garbage cans in the back yard. He heard the scratching and spitting and the howling of he didn't know how many cats outside. Now that the frightening noise of the fireworks was over they had left their hiding-places and were once more holding forth.

He sat up in bed, tense, waiting for Mr Massey's window to jerk open and the jug to be emptied or an old boot hurled.

But nothing happened.

He heard the creaking of the mattress as Mr Massey moved in bed but there was no other sound. And in a little while the night prowlers left the yard in peace.

Ginger lay down again very puzzled. He was sure Mr Massey must have heard the noise. Why had he done nothing? He thought about it for a long time and could come to only one conclusion. Miss Pilgrim. He smiled sleepily. She must have made Mr Massey change his mind. Something in her face or her voice or maybe her handbag — or perhaps all three — must have altered Mr Massey's feelings for cats.

CHAPTER
FOUR

The day after his fourteenth birthday Ginger left school for good and started work for Mr Eccles at twelve shillings a week.

Mr Massey, encouraged by Ginger and the fact that Mr Eccles had an opening for the lad, eagerly agreed the decision. He was also encouraged by the fact that the twelve bob would help towards the boy's keep and relieve him of providing odd coppers whenever Ginger did a job for him.

Times were changing, he'd told Ginger when the decision came, and there was little future in the junk shop for a likely lad. Ginger couldn't do better than start early and learn a trade. The good days of the junk trade had passed, at any rate, on the scale that the little shop of Massey could afford to operate. Times had been all right in the days when you could swap a paper windmill for a dozen jam-jars or a toy balloon for a bundle of old clothes. But now the world was changing and folks didn't use jam-jars so much; they used tins. They had more money and their kids could buy their own windmills. As for old clothes, they used them for cleaning their motor-bikes.

But that was the tide of progress. And if you had a trade you could swim with the tide. Mr Massey wished he'd had a chance to learn a trade. He'd have been a builder. Buildings always had been wanted and always would be. You couldn't do without buildings, but you could do without old ornaments and dated magazines and all the other knick-knacks that cluttered Mr Massey's shop. But if you took up a trade and stuck to it you had nothing to fear, and security in your old age.

Ginger hadn't thought about old age or security when he'd asked Mr Eccles for the job. You didn't think about old age when you were fourteen. And he didn't know what Mr Massey meant by security. No, it was nothing to do with what Mr Massey said. He wanted to work in the joiner's shop because you made things there. Ginger thought it would be exciting to make things and get paid for making them as well. But there were other reasons, too. He liked Mr Eccles; the smell of paint and varnish. He liked the scent of newly-cut wood and the different patterns you could shape timbers into when you started the engine and used the right tool. To make it even better Mr Eccles was fond of animals. You could see that by the way he treated Jemmy. And Jemmy was another reason Ginger wanted to work there.

Mr Massey didn't know that and Ginger didn't tell him. He'd said nothing about the incident in Angel Street since the night Miss Pilgrim had returned with him to the shop and he'd left the lady and Mr Massey talking downstairs. Mr Massey hadn't said anything either. At least, not about cats. He hadn't said much about Miss Pilgrim but Ginger could see she had wrought a great change in him. The night prowlers in the back yard must have seen it, too. Mr Massey had been very pleased with the barrow when it came back beautifully repaired next day, and there'd been no hard words for Ginger for taking it in the first place.

Truly, Miss Pilgrim had worked a miracle, but how was quite beyond Ginger. He was content to leave it at that. You didn't try to explain miracles. You just accepted them. And on the Sunday when he had gone to Angel Street to tea Miss Pilgrim didn't mention it. She did say she hoped Mr Eccles had made a good job of the barrow, and Jo trusted that everything was all right with Mr Massey. But that was all.

Ginger put it down to the bunch of violets he'd taken. He'd bought them from the flower-woman in Lacey Market for threepence, out of the shilling Miss Pilgrim had given him. He knew Miss Pilgrim liked flowers because there were some on the tea-table the first day he went there; but he felt a bit silly when she kept harping on how sweet it was of him to think of her, and as if to remind him of her pleasure over tea she put the little bunch of mauve petals in a small vase of water and stood it on the table. What with all the fuss over his tiny gift, and the novelty of Mr Timothy at the table, and the little feeling of sadness because Jo was going home next day, it was not surprising no one mentioned Miss Pilgrim's miracle.

Ginger had been very sorry when he'd heard Jo was going. She lived a long way away. In a place called the Midlands. She lived with her father's sister and went to a big school. He thought it must be a college. He didn't think he'd like anyone who went to college. He'd heard of college boys and girls who looked down their noses and talked as though they had a hot lump of pease pudding in their mouths. But he liked Jo. She didn't talk like that.

He'd been sorry she was going. And Jo was sorry she'd got to leave Mr Timothy. Miss Pilgrim had been sorry, too, although she smiled bravely and told Jo she'd had a long convalescence and, after all, she had only had the measles. It wasn't very long to wait for the Christmas holidays when Aunt Flo would let her return to London for a week and they could all be together again. But Jo had pulled a wry face and had thought the holidays were ages and ages away and wasn't Aunt Ann going to be lonely? It was then that Miss Pilgrim had first suggested Ginger should call each week, to have tea with her and Mr Timothy. This had cheered Jo no end, though Ginger couldn't see why as she'd be in the Midlands; but the invitation to Sunday tea every Sunday couldn't have been a better bargain for a threepenny bunch of violets.

That first exciting afternoon had come to an end to mark the beginning of a happy routine that took Ginger to Angel Street every Sunday at four. The Christmas holidays had come and gone. So had Jo. Now his fourteenth birthday had passed and he had suddenly grown up enough to start a full day's work every day in Mr Eccles's joinery shop. But Sunday was still his day for tea in the house in Angel Street.

CHAPTER
FIVE

It was Mr Eccles who told Ginger about the facts of life. Not just those dealing with the biological functions of the sexes, but the less intimate ones to do with necessities like politics, money and dog racing. Mr Eccles knew what was going on in other countries, too, and he could tell you who was behind the latest revolution in South America and why someone called Hitler was turning Germany into a military base.

"You mark my words, me lad," he would say to Ginger, "if that there jumped-up corporal doesn't give the world a shock one of these days. He'll set light to Europe before he's finished, you see, even if he comes a cropper hi'self in doing it."

Mr Eccles read the papers when he wasn't making things. He was an avid reader of facts both in the Press and in the political and travel books he borrowed from the library. But he had no wish to take part in politics himself, beyond casting his vote, that is. Neither did he wish to subject himself to long-distance travel. The journey each day from the little terrace house in Manor Park to the shop was quite enough at his age. He just wanted to know what was going on in the world and what the world looked like.

But in spite of his awareness of events outside his shop and the fact that he was one of the most practical of all men, Mr Eccles was a dreamer. With just one dream. He wanted to return to the country. That was where his roots were.

He told no one about this secret longing. Not even Mrs Eccles, for she had lived all her life in Bow and Manor Park and wouldn't understand that kind of dream. Mrs Eccles understood only realities. If she had secret dreams at all she got them at the pictures on Saturday night. So Mr Eccles kept his dream hidden away in his head under his bowler hat. But sometimes, when he and Ginger knocked off for dinner and sat on either side of the blackened fireplace, Mr Eccles would stare into the glowing embers of wood with a sad, faraway look in his eyes, and for a little while he would seem to forget everything, even the bottle of milk stout with which he always washed down his bread and cheese or the meat pie he brought with him each day.

One such day when Ginger had made the tea to wash down his own meal of fish and chips which he bought himself twice a week as a change from the sandwiches, Mr Eccles passed him the newspaper that lay open on his lap, and pointed out a picture.

"See what it is?" Mr Eccles asked with that faraway look still in his eye.

Ginger stared at the photograph. It was a huge wooden building set over a stream. The windows in the boarded walls gaped without any glass and the timbers were rotting away. Only the wild bushes and shrubs festering around it seemed to prevent it tottering into the stream.

Ginger glanced up none the wiser.

"It's a water-mill, me lad," Mr Eccles said. "It used to grind the corn. That's the water-wheel, see?" He pointed to a collection of wooden vanes that formed the top half of a circle; the lower half was submerged in the water. "The force of the stream turns the wheel and that turns the great stones inside what grinds the corn. See?"

"Go on," said Ginger. He couldn't see.

"A bit of old England, it is, and the Powers-that-be are going to pull it down and build a new contraption on its grave. One of these new fangled pumping stations. Can you beat it? Why not build a pumping station somewhere else?"

"Why not?" said Ginger.

"That's what I'd like to know," said Mr Eccles. "That's what the Society would like to know, too, God bless 'em."

"What Society?" Ginger asked.

"Why, the Society for the Preservation of Rural Britain, o' course," said Mr Eccles. "Having a rare set-to with them officials, they are. Fair wicked, it is, what they can get away with today." Mr Eccles smoothed down his moustache which had got a bit ruffled in his excitement. "Been a lot about it in the papers and so there should be. It's a famous old mill. Been painted scores of times by famous artists for the last hundred years, and one of world renown, though I can't call him to mind at the moment." Mr Eccles snorted and made his moustache jump. "It's not the only example condemned by these interfering officials neither.

Gouging out the few memorials the country craftsmen left us, that's what they're doing, instead of preserving them for posterity."

Ginger didn't know anything about water-mills, and he didn't know who posterity was; but he thought the building in the picture would very soon fall down anyway, and he couldn't see why Mr Eccles should be so upset about it.

"D'you know much about water-mills, Mr Eccles?" he asked.

"Know much about them?" said Mr Eccles. "Why, I was born slap-bang next to one."

That was how Mr Eccles came to tell Ginger about his dream. It wasn't so much because he liked water-mills better than any other mill or any other country building, it was, he explained to Ginger, simply because he liked the countryside and all the beautiful things Nature and the country craftsmen had made. He didn't want to see the townsman's ugly blemishes littering God's landscape; not before he could get back to it. And he longed to go back to where his roots were.

He was born in the country, he told Ginger, on a gentleman's estate. His father had been a carpenter there. But the estate had been sold when the gentleman died. The land had been split up and the new owners didn't want carpenters. Because times were bad in the country then the Eccles family had come to London and his father had started the joiner's shop. And now Mr Eccles was almost as old as his father had been when he died, and here he was still in the shop in the shadow of the railway bridge and the smoke of factory chimneys. But he dreamed he'd go back one day. If he could sell his business he'd go, if he could persuade his wife. All he wished for was an acre or two, and a Jersey cow, and maybe a few chickens and a greenhouse to grow cucumbers and tomatoes, and perhaps a little stream in the distance where he could fish in his spare time, like he did when he was a boy.

Mr Eccles rambled on in a quiet voice with the faraway look in his eye and if Mr Cramthorn hadn't come in for his new back door no work would have been done in the shop that afternoon. While Mr Eccles attended to Mr Cramthorn Ginger took down the empty condensed milk tin and put it on the floor for Jemmy, who'd been lulled to sleep on a heap of shavings by the soothing tone of Mr Eccles's monologue.

For a little while Ginger watched Jemmy's rough tongue scrape the sides of the tin. He wondered if animals wished for anything apart from filling their bellies. No one else seemed to be contented with what they'd got. Mr Massey wished he'd been a builder. Mr Eccles was a sort of builder but he wished he lived in the country and had a Jersey cow. He supposed everybody wished for something. When he went back to his job of heating the glue he began to wonder what he could wish for; but he couldn't think of anything at the moment.

Ginger liked working for Mr Eccles. Mr Eccles treated him as a real grown-up. Although he realised he was only a learner and had to start at the bottom and some of the jobs weren't very interesting, he never minded because Mr Eccles had a way of giving his orders so that they weren't like orders at all. He spoke mildly in a man to man manner, and the only time Ginger felt his age was when the engine was running. Mr Eccles wouldn't let Ginger work the circular saw or the plane or the spindle that bored square holes, although he often helped Mr Eccles to work them by supporting the other end of the length of wood he was cutting, planing or boring. Mr Eccles was very strict about that. "All in good time, me lad," he would say when Ginger asked if he was ever going to learn to use them. So Ginger would hide his impatience behind a pout and try to concentrate on his job, because it was no use protesting when the engine was running and the belts were whirring and the saw was screeching.

That was the only time Mr Eccles stopped talking himself. That and when a goods train rumbled over the bridge. Although there were other occasions when the job he was doing required complete quiet and concentration. Like when he was measuring out with a set square or glueing into place the joints of a cupboard or the palings of a gate. Often, on such occasions, Ginger stood by to write down the figures Mr Eccles called out as he measured the job, or to follow him over the bench with the glue pot which he would take back to the fire and re-heat when the glue got too tacky.

Those were the times when he could closely watch the master craftsman at work. When Mr Eccles completely lost himself in his job. With his bowler hat tilted back a bit to make room for the lines of concentration on his forehead, his steel-rimmed spectacles — which he only wore when the most intricate skill was called for — half-way down his nose, and the hairs of his moustache bristling with determination, Mr Eccles was a dedicated man.

Ginger was very impressed. He watched every movement in silent awe and it was so quiet you could hear a shaving drop. They might have been right in the heart of the country, where Mr Eccles's roots were. Only the harsh clanging of a goods train as it rumbled over the bridge would break the spell, and then the whole place vibrated with strident sounds that shook the sawdust from the rafters. The silence crept closer after the train had gone, and Ginger's attention would stray to Mr Eccles's black bowler which was slowly changing colour under the descending particles of sawdust. It lay like granulated sugar over the crown and along the brim but it never reached Mr Eccles's moustache. Ginger thought he would have a bowler hat if he ever had a moustache like Mr Eccles.

It was typical of Mr Eccles's generosity that the first real thing Ginger made was something that brought no profit to the business. It was a stool for Mr Timothy. Mr Eccles agreed to deduct something from Ginger's wages for the materials, and the work was done during slack periods and in the dinner-hour. So it progressed slowly, though Ginger made sure — and so did Mr Eccles secretly — that it was ready in time for Mr Timothy's birthday.

Mr Eccles actually helped at times and always he was at hand to give professional advice. As the birthday drew near and the pieces of wood grew into the shape of a crude tripod Mr Eccles took a bigger part in its creation, cutting his dinner-hour to work on it with Ginger when the shop was busy.

Three days before delivery day the three-legged stool stood on the work bench, its varnished top glistening in the light of the naked electric bulb above it. Mr Eccles stood stroking his moustache and studying their handiwork with a critical eye.

"Should ha' been French-polished," he announced. "Like I said. Puts the finishing touch to a bit o' furniture."

"Don't see what difference that makes to a cat," Ginger said. "The look o' the thing, I mean."

"Ah, but that cat's almost human," said Mr Eccles, picking up the stool again and testing the joints.

"I know that," Ginger said. "That's why I think he'd rather not have it polished. It's safer, he won't slip."

Mr Eccles shrugged philosophically.

"It's your present," he said.

"Another thing," said Ginger. "The stool he's always used — the one Miss Pilgrim keeps the fern pot on — has got no end of polish on it and you can see all the scratches where he's had to hold on with his claws. Specially when he jumps up on to it."

"Something in that," Mr Eccles nodded. He set the stool down on the bench again and eyed it from a distance, putting his head first on one side and then on the other. "Well, you've made a good job of it, me lad," he said. "It'll be a nice surprise for them both."

Ginger glowed with pride that was quickly tempered by the truth.

"You made more of it than me," he said.

"It was your thought," said Mr Eccles. "That was the most important thing. It doesn't matter what you give or whether you make it yourself. It's just the thought of giving. That's the real gift." Mr Eccles gave a deep sigh. "Well, now, you'd better leave it in the office till Saturday. It'll be safe there. Then you can get some brown paper. You always have to wrap a present."

"Yes," said Ginger. "I know, and what about some ribbon to tie it up with?"

"Just the thing," Mr Eccles said. "Blue would look nice."

Blue it was. On Saturday morning when Ginger got to the shop he had a clean sheet of brown paper folded in his pocket and a length of blue ribbon. He put them in the office with the stool and when they knocked off at midday, Mr Eccles helped him to make a neat parcel of the present. It was awkward to wrap but when they'd finished you would never have guessed what it was inside.

CHAPTER
SIX

Mr Timothy's birthday was on the Sunday. At least, that was the official day. The actual date had never been recorded. Not even Miss Pilgrim knew with any certainty how accurately she had estimated. He had been nearly three months old when he had come to her; that was in early October, so she put his birthday towards the end of July. So long as the event was recognised what did a few days either way matter? Certainly Mr Timothy didn't mind. Whether he even knew was doubtful, but the special tin of cream and the buttered haddock must have convinced him it was somebody's birthday.

Sunday was one of those hot days you sometimes get in July in England, and although Ginger had just washed himself in a copperful of cold water, put on a clean shirt and the new suit he'd got for twenty-five shillings in Commercial Road, he was sweating by the time he got to Angel Street. He loosened his tie a bit and opened his jacket, but he didn't feel any cooler. The air itself was stuffy and gritty with the dust of the streets. Near the arches was the green-grocer's depot and the smell of horses and rotting cabbage leaves didn't make the atmosphere any lighter.

Ginger put the parcel under his other arm, not because it was heavy but because he didn't want the perspiration to stain the paper. He was glad he didn't meet anyone. They'd take him for a sissy when they saw the blue ribbon. They wouldn't understand. Only cats and girls went about with ribbons. It was a relief to lose this self-consciousness in the emptiness of the streets. Angel Street was as deserted as Colman Row and Lacey Market. The houses slumbered in the afternoon heat, their blinds drawn. It looked as if all the people had died or taken the excursion train to Southend.

When Ginger got to Miss Pilgrim's house he was still sweating. He was excited, too, which made it worse. He didn't know why he should feel so sweaty and so clammy at the same time. He thought it must be the thought of causing a surprise. Of course, it would be nice to see Jo again, and he'd never get tired of having tea with Miss Pilgrim and Mr Timothy. But it wasn't that. It was the thought of seeing their faces when the parcel was undone.

Jo must have been watching from the window. Before he even touched the knocker, she opened the door. She was all white teeth and dimples as she welcomed him in, and the second thing her eyes saw was Ginger's parcel.

"Whatever's in there?" she asked.

"It's Mr Timothy's birthday, isn't it?" said Ginger.

Jo clasped her hands together excitedly.

"Oh, Ginger!" she said. "It's a present. How lovely! What is it?"

But Ginger wasn't telling. He gave her a teasing smile and went through into the room where the table was set for tea. It was cooler here, and the smell was nice. There were red and white roses on the table and cream pastries and salmon paste sandwiches. Miss Pilgrim came in with her best china teapot. She wore a pretty, green dress with lots of white frills at the neck, and there were sparkles in her eyes.

"This minute made the tea," Miss Pilgrim said, but she was looking at Ginger's parcel. He put the parcel on the sofa and Mr Timothy poked his head out from under the table and stared as if he, too, was curious about the parcel.

Ginger stooped and swept the cat up in his arms and gently rubbed the white chin. There was a silken sheen on his black coat, and his white bib looked as if it had just been washed in Persil. The white spats were spotless, too, and the pads underneath rosy pink. His eyes were wide saucers of green and Ginger could see his own reflection in the black pupils.

Ginger didn't speak. He'd never been able to master the language Miss Pilgrim used, but he didn't need words to wish Mr Timothy a happy birthday.

"Come on, Ginger," urged Jo. "Open the parcel."

Ginger carefully put Mr Timothy in his basket and he immediately got out again and began fussing round their legs, making throaty noises that were something between a purr and a meow. Ginger picked up the parcel.

"It's a little present," he said. "For Mr Timothy." He offered it to Miss Pilgrim. "You and Jo open it."

Miss Pilgrim looked a bit flustered.

"It's so big," she said, and her eyes were moist with the kind of happiness that tears came from. "We'll open it on the sofa and Mr Timothy can help." She laid the parcel on the cushions and Jo picked up the cat and put him beside it. While Miss Pilgrim untied one ribbon bow and Jo's excited fingers fumbled with the other, Mr Timothy pawed the paper. Ginger stood watching with a broad grin, his hands clasped behind his back.

There was an exclamation of surprise when all the paper was unwrapped and they saw what it was.

"It's a stool." gasped Jo. "Specially for Mr Timothy."

Miss Pilgrim threw up her hands in delight. She picked it up very gently and stood it on the floor.

"It's beautiful," she said. "And just what he wanted." She looked at Ginger, her voice soft. "You made it with your own hands."

"Well," said Ginger. "Mr Eccles helped."

"It's a wonderful present," Jo said. "He never really had a chair of his own."

"I thought it would save moving the fern pot," said Ginger. "I hope he'll like it."

"Of course he'll like it," said Miss Pilgrim, and she put it at the table in Mr Timothy's usual place. They all looked at Mr Timothy expectantly; but he didn't get up on it. He kept fussing round its legs, his tail sticking up straight as a factory chimney. Miss Pilgrim spoke to him and patted the seat. Even this didn't make any difference. She poured out a saucerful of cream and put it on his serviette, but all he did was cry mournfully and prance faster round the legs of the stool. Then she picked him up and set him on it. He immediately jumped down again. Everyone was mystified and didn't know what to do.

"He's behaving like a spoilt baby instead of a grateful little gentleman," Miss Pilgrim said gravely. But no word or action could overcome Mr Timothy's obstinacy. The tea was getting cold, the sandwiches were beginning to lose their bloom. Even the cream pastries were drooping. In the end Miss Pilgrim had to take the potted fern off the stool in the window. It was the only way they could all sit down.

All that summer Miss Pilgrim persevered with Mr Timothy; but it was no use, he wouldn't take his place at the table on the stool that Ginger made. Jo went to Paris with her school on one of those educational holidays, but when she got back neither her aunt nor Ginger were any nearer solving the problem.

It was Mr Eccles who suggested a remedy when Ginger was talking about it for the umpteenth time one day.

"Why don't you do like I said in the first place?" he said. "French-polish it. Never did look properly finished."

"But a little thing like that can't make no difference," said Ginger.

"Never mind. Try it," said Mr Eccles. "Cats are fussy creatures. They get into certain habits and nothing'll change 'em. They're like women, always particular over little things."

"Never should have thought he'd rather have a slippery seat, like the fern pot stool," Ginger said mournfully; but he borrowed his present back and under the watchful eye of Mr Eccles French-polished it. It was wonderful the difference it made; not only to the stool, but to Mr Timothy.

Ginger would never forget the day he took it back. The last Sunday in September, it was. He only wished Jo could have been there to see it.

Miss Pilgrim took the stool and casually placed it next to the one on which the fern pot stood, near the window. They looked almost identical now. She went into the kitchen for the saucer of fish, Mr Timothy fussing around her feet. She put this on the serviette and poured milk into the second saucer. Mr Timothy trotted excitedly up and down and round and under the table, yelling with impatience. Then Miss Pilgrim moved the stool Ginger had made to the table. She and the boy stood back and watched hopefully. But this time there was no nonsense. No hesitation even. Mr Timothy leapt straight on to it and settled comfortably on the polished seat. He looked round at Ginger and his mistress, anxiously imploring them to sit down so that he could start. Miss Pilgrim nodded and he began eating his fish.

Ginger and Miss Pilgrim looked at each other helplessly. It seemed too good to be true. They sat down themselves, quietly, lest they should break the spell.

"Would you believe it!" said Miss Pilgrim at length, her eyes glowing on Mr Timothy. "Swank, that's what it is. Wanted his present polished, if you please."

"Just shows you," said Ginger; but he wasn't sure what it did show you except, of course, that Mr Eccles had been right.

"I must write and tell Jo," Miss Pilgrim said. "She'll be so glad to know we're all settled at last."

Ginger nodded. His mouth was full of currant bread. And he was very happy.

Jo didn't come in the Christmas holidays. She had the mumps. Jo's father, who was on leave from the Merchant Navy, sent them Jo's love and wishes and said how much she missed them all. Ginger spent a whole evening writing a little letter to her which Miss Pilgrim was going to enclose with her own.

Ginger shared the Christmas with Miss Pilgrim and her cat and Mr Massey whose sister at Leytonstone had sent him a Christmas pudding. But when Ginger was round at the house in Angel Street it didn't seem like holiday time somehow without Jo. He wasn't interested in girls. He never thought he'd ever miss one. But he missed Jo. He didn't know why. Unless it was because he knew Miss Pilgrim and Mr Timothy missed her, too.

He thought Jo was a good sport, and never showed off about her education, though he wished she didn't know so much. Her father, too, was clever. He was something big on a liner. High up. On the bridge, Ginger supposed. Like Ginger, Jo hadn't got a mother. She lived with her Aunt Flo and a parrot. Parrots and cats didn't get on too well and Jo preferred fur to feathers. That was why she liked coming to Angel Street. Mr Timothy was the attraction, although as she grew older there were other attractions, too.

It seemed to Ginger a long time to Easter, but when at last the holiday came, there was Jo. All smiles and dimples and fluffy dark hair. Just like she'd been the last time he saw her the previous summer. Yet, not quite the same somehow. There was something a bit different about her; as if she'd suddenly grown a bit older than Ginger when he knew she was nearly a year younger than he was.

Mr Timothy didn't notice any difference. Jo still got down on the floor like a little girl and played with the cat, rolling him over on the rug and tickling his chest till his tongue peeped out of his mouth and he rocked with laughter. She still played games with him with a paper ball or a piece of string. But she'd changed just a little, Ginger knew. She unsettled him a bit. He didn't feel so sure he was right when he told her anything. Perhaps it was just because of her education. Or perhaps he was changing, too. But Miss Pilgrim didn't notice anything, except, a little sadly inside her, she noticed they were both growing up and soon they would fly away.

Easter Monday was a warm, sunny day and it was Miss Pilgrim who suggested that Jo and Ginger should have an outing for a change. Why didn't they go up the river to Hampton Court? she said. They didn't have to spend all their time with her and Mr Timothy. They could come back to a late tea. It would make a lovely day for them. Miss Pilgrim insisted so much, they went. Jo in a bright primrose dress with a light open coat. Ginger in his Sunday suit with a collar and tie.

They had a lovely day. And in spite of the little ache that Ginger felt because Jo was not quite the same, he was proud to be with her. She looked so nice, and everyone on the boat kept glancing at her. Although he knew she must be used to travelling about, she pretended she wasn't. She let him get the tickets, and she asked all the questions. But she didn't ask for the liquorice allsorts or the lemonade; she waited till he got around to them. She followed Ginger's lead just like any nice girl would who was nearly a year younger, even if she was a bit older in other ways.

It was Ginger who led her off the boat and in and out of the Maze, but when they studied the famous palace, it was Jo who told him its history. He couldn't remember who Cardinal Wolsey was or when Henry the Eighth reigned; but he thought it was that Henry who had such a lot of wives. Jo remembered everything. That was the trouble, he thought, her education. He felt so — so blooming small. It didn't matter so much when you were kids, or if he'd been the girl and she'd been the boy, it would have been all right. But as it was — well, you noticed it. Still, it was a lovely day.

The Sunday after Jo went back Ginger put his problem to Miss Pilgrim. Miss Pilgrim understood. She was like Mr Eccles for understanding things. Perhaps she had a secret dream, too. She told Ginger not to worry. You didn't get all your education out of history books, she told him. Learning about life was the most important thing and you didn't begin that education till you'd left school. And you never stopped learning.

"Of course," Miss Pilgrim went on, "Josephine's a bright girl, but she's no cleverer than you." She stopped stroking Mr Timothy's head for a moment and smiled at Ginger. Mr Timothy snuggled further into her lap and closed his eyes.

"Go on," said Ginger. "She's miles ahead of me. She seems so — well — so used to things, if you know what I mean."

Miss Pilgrim smiled again. Mr Timothy seemed to be smiling, too. In his sleep of course.

"I know what you mean," Miss Pilgrim said. "Most girls of her age seem like that to boys of your age. It's just the way they're made."

"But education helps," said Ginger.

"Oh, yes. It helps. A good school, good friends, success in exams and on the sports field gives you confidence. And if you want to be a success in life that's something you must have, confidence. But there're other things, too."

"Brains," said Ginger. "Jo's got brains."

"We've all got a brain," Miss Pilgrim said. "Whether it's noticeable or not depends on if and how we use it. But it's what is in your heart that matters most." Miss Pilgrim put the sleeping cat gently into his basket. "Now," she said to Ginger. "Go and put the kettle on while I set the table, and we'll talk about education over tea."

That was the talk that led Ginger to evening classes. Not classes in geography or history; he was to learn those subjects from the books Miss Pilgrim recommended he should read; but courses in English and mathematics and drawing, too, because he'd made up his mind now to be a draughtsman.

Mr Eccles agreed with Miss Pilgrim that Ginger should go far if he studied hard enough and, after all, as Mr Eccles said, a clever young lad didn't want to stop in the joinery shop making window sashes all his life, not if he'd got a gift for designing them.

So Ginger began to study hard. He got down to English grammar. He started to read the books his teacher recommended as well as borrowing those that Mr Eccles and Miss Pilgrim thought were good for him. He'd always liked drawing and the mathematics didn't seem so difficult when you studied them voluntarily. Of course, he was slow at first, but by the end of term he thought he was making good progress. He was looking forward to testing out his knowledge on Jo when she came back to Angel Street.

But Jo didn't come back. Her father took her to Australia on his liner. He thought there was going to be war in Europe.

CHAPTER
SEVEN

It wasn't easy to say who missed Jo the most in the house in Angel Street. If she hadn't been a frequent visitor she had appeared regularly each holiday time — except the Christmas she had the mumps — and after she'd gone back on each occasion Miss Pilgrim and Ginger knew that she was only a school term away. But Australia was a different cup of tea. It was a world away. Still, there was nothing you could do about it and, as Mr Eccles said, the rumblings in Europe that began to make themselves heard soon after Jo sailed only went to show what a sensible man Jo's father was.

Jo wrote long letters about her new life to her aunt and Ginger, and over tea on Sundays they would read them aloud to each other, addressing to Mr Timothy those remarks which alluded to him. Jo sent some snapshots, too; but neither these nor her letters could make up for her absence, and so far as Mr Timothy was concerned they made no difference at all. Physical contact was the only thing he could appreciate. He missed her voice, the fuss she made of him, the games she played with him, and he couldn't understand why she never came. He didn't know anything about Europe or Australia.

The ominous cloud spreading its eagle wings beyond the North Sea never cast its shadow over Angel Street. Most folk didn't look that way while the sun was shining. Except Mr Eccles. He voiced his anxious opinions with mounting intensity, but he was well-read and could read the writing on the wall. Ginger never paid much attention. He was busy with his education. And if Miss Pilgrim thought much about it at all she kept her thoughts to herself.

Ginger still went to tea every Sunday and he and Miss Pilgrim talked about his work and his studies. They fussed Mr Timothy and thought about Jo. They continued to read her letters to each other, although as time went on Ginger got a bit shy about reading aloud some of the things Jo wrote, and he left them out. Miss Pilgrim understood and said nothing. She could read between the breaks.

About the time Jo finished her schooling in far-away Australia and went into a training hospital in Sydney, Ginger was talking to Mr Eccles about changing his job. Rather, it was Mr Eccles doing the talking. It was his idea. He had been thinking about Ginger's future for a while, though as things were, he didn't give much for the chances of anyone's future. Still, you had to go on hoping and praying and working and leave the rest to God and the Government.

Mr Eccles thought Ginger had made great strides in his education and this particular aptitude he had for drawing could no longer be ignored. He thought it was time Ginger looked round for a proper outlet for his talents and, of course, better wages than Mr Eccles would ever be able to afford. Miss Pilgrim had often given Ginger similar advice, so it wasn't Mr Eccles's lecture that decided events. It was what Mr Eccles did. He happened to meet a man he knew who knew a man who happened to mention that the Kelly Construction Company were expanding down at West Drayton and were looking for one or two embryo draughtsmen for their drawing office. When things happen like that it's not just coincidence; it's Fate. And you have to accept it. Ginger did. One bright May morning he went across London to West Drayton for the interview, and got the job.

It was sad leaving Mr Eccles and saying good-bye to Jemmy; yet it was really Mr Eccles's fault.

Ginger soon settled down in his new job. But he couldn't settle down in West Drayton. He had to live there all the week. His lodgings were cheap, but his landlady was a tartar. She was skimpy with the food, so strict about the house he couldn't wipe his boots on the front door mat, not before he'd cleaned them on some sacking in the shed. And no dog or cat could be tempted to come within yards of the place. It was funny how you could have two people of the same sex and age as Miss Pilgrim and his landlady, living alone in the same sort of house, who could yet be so totally different. But Ginger never said anything when he went back to Button Row at the week-ends. He just thought that was life, and he was learning about it. He might have told Mr Eccles if he'd met him, but Mr Eccles always went home to Manor Park from noon Saturday till Monday morning, which was very awkward for meeting. Of course, Mr Eccles knew how Ginger was getting on because Miss Pilgrim told him. Ginger still went to tea with her and Mr Timothy on Sundays.

Ginger travelled back to Button Row every week-end and it was surprising the change you could see in people after only five days. Mr Massey, for instance. Ginger couldn't help noticing how old he had suddenly become, as if a year of his life was passing between Ginger's visits. His face was more drawn and lined. His body thinner. Shrivelling up, he seemed to be. Ginger knew it was his cough doing it. It was more frequent. More violent. It rent and shook him so much it seemed you could hear all his bones rattling. Whenever Ginger had mentioned a doctor Mr Massey had been contemptuous. He was an obstinate man. Independent. He thought he could cure himself with medicine from the chemist. It took him a long time to realise his treatment had failed.

One week-end after Ginger had been working in West Drayton about a couple of months, Mr Massey came out with the news that he'd seen the doctor and been to the hospital, too. They were sitting at breakfast in the kitchen behind the shop on the Sunday morning. Ginger stopped eating, he was so surprised and relieved.

"The doctor sent me to the hospital to have one of these 'ere X-Rays," Mr Massey said.

"X-Rays?" said Ginger. "That's what Jo's doing, learning about X-Rays."

Mr Massey blinked his watery eyes over the rim of his thick china tea mug.

"Who's Jo?" he asked.

"Josephine. You remember, Miss Pilgrim's niece. Went to Australia. She's training in a hospital there, learning to X-Ray people."

"Ah," said Mr Massey wondrously. "She must be a clever one. It was a man what worked the machine on me."

"What did they tell you at the hospital?" Ginger asked.

"Nothing," Mr Massey said. "They never do. See your own doctor, they said. I saw him Thursday. The report'd come through." He put down his mug and wiped his nose. When he spoke again his voice trembled a bit. "I got to go away. For treatment. A sanatorium, the doctor called it. Near the sea. It's gonna take a long time."

Ginger smiled to comfort the old man, but his eyes were smarting. Mr Massey looked so frail and pitiable. Even the china mug seemed too heavy for him with the tea in it. Mr Massey had been a good man, a just man. Deep down inside him the warm glow of kindness had always been there. If on occasion it didn't shine very bright, the cough was to blame.

Ginger tried to look cheerful.

He said: "I'll come and see you. What difference does time make so long as it does the trick? You'll soon get better with proper treatment."

"It's gonna be very long, the doctor said."

"So you'll have a good rest. You've earned it. And you'll come back fresh as new paint to start again."

"Not 'ere, I shan't," Mr Massey said slowly. "I'll never come back 'ere. I've sold the place to Isaacs."

"What — the pawnbroker?" Ginger was surprised. He

hadn't thought about what would happen to the business.

"Ay. What good it'll do him, I don't know. He done it as a favour, no two ways about that. What else could you do wi' the place? Me away, and for a long time. It's a weight off me mind."

"So what will you do when you're better?"

"Retire," said Mr Massey, vaguely looking through the wall of the kitchen into the future. "My sister wants me to live with her."

Ginger was glad Mr Massey had made plans. It was nice to know his sister was waiting for him. Ginger felt that was a weight off his own mind.

"Mr Isaacs takes over next Saturday," Mr Massey said, looking round the kitchen and through the door into the shop. "So if there's anything you want you'd best mark it up now." He suddenly opened his mouth and gulped, then started to cough into his handkerchief. The cough rasped right through his body. Each spasm brought a fleck of colour to his pinched white face and his eyes ran. Ginger could feel the torture of it. At last it stopped and Mr Massey wiped his eyes.

"So you see how it is, me boy. You'd best look round this morning. Take just what you want."

Ginger stared at the oilcloth on the table.

"There's nothing I want," he said, "'cept for you to get better."

It was very sad saying good-bye to Mr Massey. Much worse than the time he left Mr Eccles. Ginger knew that Mr Massey was ill, and that makes all the difference when you're saying good-bye. But he promised he'd go and see him at the sanatorium after Mr Massey had settled down. The Kelly Construction Company were giving him a week's holiday in September and that's when he'd make his visit. It wasn't very long to wait. And it was something they could both look forward to.

Ginger told Miss Pilgrim about it when he called that afternoon. He didn't stop to tea. He thought he should spend the rest of his time with Mr Massey. Miss Pilgrim thought so, too. The news upset her but she was sure that going to the sanatorium was the best thing that could happen for Mr Massey. He'd be well looked after and she had no doubts that in time they would get him well again. She thought when Ginger saw him in September the patient would already be on the mend. She told Ginger not to worry; now her house was his home whenever he chose to come.

Ginger's mind was much easier when he went back to West Drayton that night. He began to count the days to September. But he never got his holiday. That was the September the war came.

CHAPTER
EIGHT

The Stukas were at it again. In the distance. Ginger could hear the familiar whine as they went into their dive. Some poor blighters were going to cop it back along the road. A road littered with panic-stricken refugees and dishevelled Froggies; flanked with knocked-out tanks and gutted lorries. Troops moving up. Troops moving back. Lost troops, without leadership. Confusion. Refugees. Everywhere. Handcarts, donkey-carts, prams and barrows, piled high with the remnants of homes blown to rubble.

That was the road. It made you sick to see it. Not in your stomach; you didn't have a stomach any more. In your heart.

The sergeant had turned off the road a mile back. He thought they'd stand a better chance in the lane. It was little more than a cart-track, but there were few obstructions. Anything was better than the road. So long as you were going west. So long as the car kept going. It was a battered two-seater with its back shot off. French, the sergeant said it was. Ginger thought the sergeant should know. He'd practically put it together. That's what he was doing when Ginger and Shanks had found him. Up in Belgium.

It had brought them so far. Through the desolate, desiccated wastes of western Belgium into the fields of France. The sergeant was good at siphoning petrol from the tanks of abandoned vehicles. He seemed good at most things. Ginger didn't know his name. He ran a garage in Civvy Street. On the Bath Road it was, near Reading. He talked so much about it you'd have thought he was driving there. But sometimes it kept your mind off other things. You could see the garage clearly, the way the sergeant put it, just off the busy road, its three red pumps gleaming in the morning sunshine on the concrete apron. The little office and workshop behind. The sergeant's assistant in blue overalls, serving the petrol and checking the customers' tyres. You could see the sergeant in his glory underneath some disembowelled car over the workshop pit. And behind it all the little bungalow and the sound of a vacuum cleaner and kiddies' laughter. It was a good business. The sergeant hadn't had it long when the war came.

The car wasn't built for three, but they didn't notice it. Shanks was in the middle. He was a thin, studious bloke. He was going to be an accountant. He'd passed two exams. There was only one more to go and he'd get letters after his name. He'd have an office to himself and a secretary. But that was in the future. The other side of the Channel. It was a long way to go. Shanks never said much about it. He never said much at all. Ginger could tell by the look in his eyes where his thoughts were. His wife was going to have a baby.

Shanks had had no news from home for a week. Neither had anyone else. He and Ginger had been together in the same unit. Only one of the many units broken up, scattered, overrun by Jerry's fast-moving armoured columns. Cut up and cut off, it had been every man for himself in their escape from death or capture. They'd travelled together without a gun, a raincoat over their tattered uniforms. That's how they'd found the sergeant. In the cartshed of a deserted Belgian farm sweating into place the bits and pieces that would carry him to some British post.

The journey was a continuation of the nightmare that had begun a lifetime ago. Day and night. The stopping and starting, taking cover, strafed, bombed and bilked, keeping the car moving somehow in the great stream westward. But the sergeant's spirit never flagged. Nothing could get him down. If he was lost he knew where he was going. He meant to get there. Ginger thought it must be the garage on the Bath Road. It was a magnet; a power that was the source of the sergeant's endurance.

It was early afternoon when they were forced into cover again. Three Me's came down out of the sun. The sergeant heard them before they dived. They were too high to identify, but he knew. He skidded the car off the track and up under a line of willow trees edging a pool. The three men jumped out and ran under the trees round the pool and dropped into a ditch a few yards beyond.

They were opposite a deserted farm cottage only a hundred feet away. It had white-washed walls and the door and window frames were painted green. The garden was shady with flowers and trees. If it hadn't been for the hole in the roof and the broken windows you might have been in England waiting for a pretty girl to come out and invite you in to tea.

They flung themselves low in the wet ditch as the planes

screamed over, guns rattling above the engines' roar. A line of fire streaked across the ground from the ditch to the cottage. Cannon shell and bullet tore into the building. The walls gaped open. The roof sagged. A nearby straw stack suddenly burst into flame.

The planes wheeled upwards. The smell of burning reeked the air. The ditch and shrubs lay flattened and scorched, the ground pockmarked with scars.

"The bastards haven't finished yet," the sergeant said. His face was grimy with dust and sweat; but his voice didn't waver. He peered up into the sky, shading the bitter determination in his eyes with his hand. "Trigger-happy, they are. Let go at anything. Even a bloody rabbit. They'd turn tail if they saw a Hurricane." He spoke with conviction; but he knew that Jerry was tougher than that.

Shanks knew it, too. But he said nothing. He was lying on his stomach sloped against the bank of the ditch, staring at the smoking cottage. His face was grey; a blank mask of hopeless despair.

Ginger tipped back his helmet. His hand was shaking. His throat was parched, gritty, as though he'd swallowed a mouthful of burning sand. It was always like that when he was waiting. That was the worst of all; the inaction; waiting to be shot up with nothing to return the fire. If only you could do something . . . That was when he saw it.

A cat. Grey, it was, like a lithe shadow, leaping from the broken window of the cottage on to the splintered door lying across the ground. It crouched there, bewildered, terrified, the stench of fire and destruction glazing it to a piece of statuary. It was a rind of a creature. But it was alive. Deserted. Left to face whatever came, alone.

Ginger suddenly thought of the fireworks in Angel Street.

He could see Mr Timothy crouching there . . . And he was climbing out of the ditch, running across the open ground. He was unconscious of the danger, the target he offered. All the tension had gone. He knew what he must do, and every fear and feeling was submerged beneath the one objective; he had to save the cat.

He ran fast, bent low. He was well in the open before his companions realised he had gone. The sergeant shouted. He couldn't understand. He didn't know why Ginger had suddenly broken cover. But Shanks did. He'd been looking that way, his eyes just above the level of the ditch.

"It's a cat, Sarge," he said. His voice trembled with excitement. "He's gone to fetch the little blighter."

"Come back!" the sergeant roared. But he knew it was too late. The Me's screamed down again. He pulled Shanks into the bottom of the ditch. "The bloody young fool." The sergeant's voice broke. "Chucking his life away like that."

It was the first time Ginger had disobeyed an order. He'd heard the sergeant's shouts, but they meant nothing to him. Nothing could have shaken his resolve. It was a mission he'd done before.

He was close to the cat when he heard the planes dive. The creature didn't move. His eyes were wide, orange-coloured, as if the burning stack flamed in them. The animal crouched back, his muscles coiled to spring, but he must have known why Ginger came.

Ginger swept him up and lunged to the side of the cottage, throwing himself and the cat down into a cluster of raspberry canes alongside an outbuilding. The whistle and crack of bullets and shell and the roar of engines was an ear-splitting inferno all around him. The ground

64

suddenly trembled and a deafening explosion rent the air. Earth and dust showered over him. Flying metal clanged against the building and thudded to the ground. A cloud of black smoke surged up from somewhere behind and there was the crackle and snap of flame eating wood.

The dust settled. And suddenly there was silence. Ominous, heavy with the stench of petrol and smoke. The faint crackle of fire died away.

Ginger looked up, dazed to see the building beside him still there. The cat thrust himself against Ginger's body as if to hide from stark reality. Ginger lay there, stroking the matted fur, trying to collect himself, wondering about the strange numbness in his leg.

It was a long time before he moved. He wanted to be sure. But the planes didn't come back. Neither did Shanks or the sergeant call or come in search of him. His leg felt queer. A wave of fear and sickness passed through him. He hugged the cat to his chest. The little creature was a comfort; something to hold on to. They were grateful for each other.

Ginger started to raise himself. Slowly, cautiously. It wasn't the enemy this time; it was his leg. He got to his feet, holding the cat in the crook of one arm, supporting himself against the wall with the other. His leg was numb, but he knew his foot was on the ground. He could feel his toes when he moved them in his boot. But his leg felt funny. And there was blood on his trousers.

He limped slowly back towards the ditch. But the ditch wasn't there. He couldn't understand it. He turned to focus the ruin of the cottage and his eyes followed a hazy course across the ground. He couldn't measure the distance any more; but he knew where the ditch should be. But it had gone and in its place were furrows of fresh earth, jagged scraps of metal, broken branches and sods of turf. Further along there was half a plane's wing lying battered against the sawn off branches of a tree. A chunk of swastika-covered fuselage near the smouldering stack. There was no trace of Shanks or the sergeant. It took him a long time to realise that the crashing plane had ploughed the ditch into his companions' grave.

The cat began to purr in his arms. Ginger felt sick again, and now there was a throbbing pain in his leg. He felt cold and hot and then cold again. He wanted to lie down and close his eyes and shut out the horror of it. He could see the sergeant's garage on the Bath road. He could see Shanks's wife with her baby. But he'd never see the sergeant and Shanks again. He would have been with them but for the cat.

His eyes smarted and his face was wet and sticky with tears and dust. He knew he was weak, growing weaker. Only the cat was strong. Ginger could feel the animal's head pushing against his chest. The deep throaty purr shut out all other sound. It might have been Mr Timothy. Ginger closed his eyes . . . It was Mr Timothy. And there was Miss Pilgrim smiling across the tea table and offering him another piece of cake. And Jo was there, too, in a light primrose dress and everyone was looking at her. But she was looking only at Ginger . . .

Ginger rubbed his eyes and the acrid smell was back. He could see the mutilated hedges and the ground in front of him. But he felt stronger. He knew he could go on. He had to go on. It was his duty. And there was the cat.

He started towards the willows. His leg was agony but

somehow he managed to drag it along, the cat still clutched in his arm. He got round the pool to the other side. The car was still under the trees. It was a slow, dizzy business climbing in, but he had the cat to think about. Ginger got him settled on the passenger seat and eventually slid down beside him. The cat looked like a good traveller. He sat with his stringy tail wrapped round his front paws and his back leaning against the torn seat-rest. Ginger wondered if the car would start. When he got his breath he pressed the starter. The engine stuttered, then throbbed into life. You could always rely on the sergeant.

Ginger reached the air strip at dusk. He was all in. His head drooping, his body sagging, but when the sentries lifted him out they had to use some force to release his hands from the steering wheel. He was semi-conscious and they took him into the guardroom tent and called for the medical orderlies and a stretcher. They were so busy with Ginger they didn't see the cat on the passenger seat jump out the other side when they opened the door.

The medical officer came with the orderlies, dressed Ginger's wound and gave him an injection, and the orderlies took him across to the sick bay on the stretcher. Ginger slowly opened his eyes as they put him on the bed. He suddenly realised he'd left the car — and the cat. With an extraordinary surge of strength he jolted upright, scaring the two men.

"Where's the cat?" Ginger demanded.

The orderlies were astounded.

"What cat, mate?" the senior asked gently.

"The grey cat. The one that saved my life," Ginger said.

"Ho, that one," said the orderly with a sly wink at his

assistant. "Don't you worry about 'im, mate. 'E's gorn to the cook-'ouse. Jock's giving 'im a feed."

Ginger lay back and closed his eyes. There was a faint smile on his lips.

The second orderly grinned at his companion.

"Queer the way they git these 'allucinations, ain't it?" he muttered. "I've heard o' them cases afore. Swear blind, they do, that some animal's saved their life. Bloody mystery, I reckon." He went on talking. But Ginger didn't hear him.

He was asleep.

CHAPTER
NINE

The major looked a bully. He reminded Ginger of the fat boy with the fireworks in Angel Street all those years ago. Just how many years ago? It wasn't easy to tell. So much had happened in between.

Ginger had grown up a lot since then. He'd learned a lot about life, and something about death. He'd been one of the tattered survivors on the trek back to Dunkirk. But he'd missed the great sea evacuation. They had flown him from the airstrip in France to the hospital in England. The wound in his leg had healed quickly, but the wound in his mind was a different picture. He'd never forget the experience, the last one he remembered of France. He'd never forget the sergeant or Shanks or the lean, grey cat.

He'd spent his sick leave at Miss Pilgrim's house. He'd talked to Mr Eccles in the old joinery shop and had seen Mr Massey, now living with his sister. Not in Leytonstone. She'd been evacuated to a village in North Essex. Mr Massey was almost well again, his cough practically gone, and he and his sister were happy together.

Staying with Miss Pilgrim and Mr Timothy and seeing Mr Eccles and Mr Massey, did Ginger no end of good. It helped to dim all the unpleasant things and dry up the scars in his mind. He was just a little sad sometimes that he didn't know the sergeant's garage or where Shanks's wife lived. But when you thought about it maybe it was as well. If you knew, you'd want to call and that might make things worse. It wouldn't help the women. It wouldn't do a bit of good to let them see the one that got away. And how could you tell them about the cat? They wouldn't understand. He couldn't understand himself. But Miss Pilgrim seemed to understand when he'd told her, though she didn't try to explain it.

After his leave Ginger was posted to Scotland on a refresher course, and the bully was his CO. But he wasn't a bully really. He was only doing his job for the duration. Off-duty he was quite human.

Ginger enjoyed the army in Scotland so far as it was possible to enjoy being a soldier when you were nearly a draughtsman. The camp was small, near the sea and the blokes were good company. The course was pretty wearying, but it didn't rain much although they were on the west coast and it was July. Miss Pilgrim thought it would be cold so far north and he hadn't been there a fortnight when she sent him a pair of long woollen stockings and a new balaclava. There was a new snap of

Mr Timothy, too, in the same parcel. It was the best one Ginger had seen. Mr Timothy was sitting on his stool in the back garden right next to the run Mr Eccles had made. He looked as well-bred as ever. Proud, indifferent, as if he was waiting for the judge to hand him the bouquet at a beauty show. It was much better than the first photograph Miss Pilgrim had sent which he had lost with a lot of other things in France.

Ginger would always remember that day in the billet when Miss Pilgrim's first letter arrived. It was soon after he had joined the army. He sat on his bed, slit the envelope and tugged out the letter and the photograph fell on the floor. Sparkes picked it up. Corporal Sparkes, it was. He thought it was a picture of a girl. The other blokes in the billet crowded round. "What's she like? Let's have a squint," they chanted. He could recall all their faces as Sparkes held up the photo and rocked with laughter. "Why," he roared, "it's a bloody great cat!" And he clicked his fingers at Ginger, calling: "Puss, puss, puss." And the others took up the chorus.

Ginger could smile now, but he was fuming at the time, and he would have biffed Sparkes one if he hadn't been a corporal. He was careful with his letters after that, but never lived it down till he was posted from the unit.

Ginger tucked the photo of Mr Timothy into his wallet along with the snap of Miss Pilgrim and the latest picture of Jo. He often took out his snaps and looked at them, but more often he looked at Jo. She was worth looking at. Even Mr Timothy, appealing as he was, couldn't compete now. Jo had grown up fast since those earlier snaps she'd sent. Specially in this one. She was on some beach near Sydney, in a white swimsuit. She had a wonderful figure and you could see how tanned she was when you looked at the swimsuit. The wind was blowing through her dark hair and she'd still got her dimples. It was a lovely picture. The only thing that spoiled it was the man in the background. He was a long way back, but he was looking at Jo. Ginger didn't like him, but he couldn't cut him out of the picture without disfiguring Jo.

He'd written and told her to send another photograph, but that took time. Australia was a world away and there was a war on. Letters between them were often delayed, and some didn't reach their destination at all. And what with him moving around so much he'd thought it best if Jo wrote to Angel Street. Miss Pilgrim sent the letters on to him, and her house became a sort of private post office. But there were long gaps between and Ginger knew Jo had other duties to perform besides writing letters and being photographed.

It was the letter from Miss Pilgrim at the end of July that brought the bad news about Jo's father. His liner had gone down. Torpedoed. Jo's father wasn't among the survivors. He had stayed with the ship. Jo had written a short brave letter to Miss Pilgrim, air mail, and she'd ended up by saying she was coming home. That was all, but it was enough to send waves of excitement and anxiety through Ginger. Excitement because he would be seeing her again; anxiety for her safety. She was coming by sea; probably already on her way. He didn't know the name of the ship. And Jerry was sinking ships wholesale. You couldn't find out what happened or where, or which ships they were. That was security; don't tell the enemy. Ginger knew that; but the suspense was awful. He tried to lose himself completely in the refresher course, but the thought of Jo's voyage was always there, nagging at the back of his mind.

Towards the end of August his anxiety was removed by a letter with the London post-mark, for the envelope was addressed in Jo's handwriting. She had arrived safely. She was staying with her aunt in Angel Street for a few days and then going to a hospital in Hertfordshire. She told him Aunt Ann had been ill for the past month, but was getting better now. She'd overtaxed herself, the doctor had said. What with her needlework and knitting at home and all her voluntary work for the WVS outside, it was no wonder. Jo was trying to get her and Mr Timothy to spend a few days in Hertfordshire when she was quite better. "But you know what Aunt Ann is," Jo wrote, "she doesn't really want to leave her home and she thinks that once I get her into the country I'll make her stay. She thinks up all manner of excuses. If it isn't her work and responsibilities to the WVS, it's Mr Timothy, he wouldn't be happy in a strange place or, how can she leave her house and not know what's going on. And so on. She has promised to spend a week-end with me later, when I'm settled and can find her accommodation, but I think she ought to move right out of London. I wonder if you could persuade her . . .?"

Ginger looked up from the letter and stared through the window of his billet across the spur of rock to the sea. *Could he persuade her!* Time and time again he'd tried to persuade Miss Pilgrim to move, but nothing he had urged or threatened could budge her resolve. She was determined no one was going to drive her from her own home. So what could you do? If Jo could get her out of the house for a week-end even, it would be a miracle. And wasn't it just typical of Miss Pilgrim that she'd said nothing in her letters about her illness? He had wondered why recent letters had been so short and the writing a bit shaky. He never dreamed she was ill. He thought she'd written at the end of the day and was tired.

Ginger read the letter through twice, and the last bit three times, for that's where Jo had said how much she was looking forward to seeing him again, and when was he getting some leave? Ginger had to write and explain that there was no leave till the end of the course which had three more weeks to run. Then he would be posted to a unit in the south. He was due for leave as soon as he got there. He was looking forward to seeing Jo and he hoped they would all have a grand reunion at the house in Angel Street.

His letter was long and cheerful, and any girl as old as Jo was in her ways could make the letter even longer if she read between the lines. Ginger wrote to Miss Pilgrim, too, but he didn't say anything about her illness; he was afraid she might be annoyed with Jo for telling him. So he asked after Mr Timothy instead and whether he had remembered Jo. He ended up by repeating the bit about the grand reunion.

Ginger had waited so long for such an occasion that a further three weeks sounded like no time at all in comparison, yet from the very next day it began to seem endless. The strict camp routine suddenly became more petty and irritating, the weather changed, and everything was wet, steamy, enveloped in mist. When it wasn't a sea mist it was a Scotch mist, and when it wasn't either it just rained. The skies were overcast day and night, and sometimes the clouds hung so low you could have thrown your forage cap into their black, ugly bellies. But the three weeks eventually got to two, then one, and Ginger's spirits began to rise in proportion.

He had received another letter from Jo. She was taking up her radiography post in Hertfordshire and would write him from there as soon as she settled in. She would come up to London on her first off-duty day as soon as he came on leave. Miss Pilgrim had written, too, reminding him that it wasn't many days now before they would all be together again, just like old times, she said. As if he needed reminding!

He couldn't even concentrate on letters any more. His mind was already groping a week ahead. But the week between had to be reckoned with. That was the week the bombing of the capital began. The week that Ginger and the rest of the world heard that London could take it.

CHAPTER
TEN

Ginger reached Victoria at midday. All the way up through the Sussex countryside from Ternfield he'd been fighting back the dark thoughts created by Miss Pilgrim's silence. Neither she nor Jo had replied to his last letter.

Ginger had written briefly from Scotland a couple of days before he left; nearly a week ago, that was. He had given them his new address at Ternfield hoping he would have had a letter before he started his leave. But there had been nothing. He didn't even know if Jo was still at the house or if she had taken up her post at the hospital. He thought she must have done; but why hadn't she written and told him where it was? Somewhere in Hertfordshire, that's all he knew.

Ginger took the Metropolitan Line to Aldgate, so he didn't see the destruction in the City. He got the No. 15 bus down Commercial Road. He rode on top so he could see around; but his mind kept riding ahead of him. As the bus passed a gap in the buildings flanking the road his mind would be jerked back to the moment. He would see the ugly gash, the heap of rubble, the scarred and scorched bits of timber. It was a familiar sight. But it was different somehow. This was London, where his home was. But people carried on. Business as usual.

The road was crowded as it always had been. There were more uniforms about, that was the difference. The warden and the firemen could be seen as often as the police. Women still stood in two's and three's gossiping on street corners or peering at the stills outside the picture house. They wore scarves over their heads and carried shopping bags. Their faces were pinched and white, their eyes red-rimmed, puffy; as though they'd been up all night every night in Anderson shelters. The pubs and cafés were open. Outside some stood small groups of men, talking in the sun. Their faces, too, were colourless, but they looked cheerful. Ginger wondered how they felt inside. They were tough, these folk. They could take it. They'd got guts. But they'd got feelings, too.

Ginger got off near the station, followed the road for a few yards, then turned up Silent Street. A long way behind him came the faint hoot of a river tug. Soon, the sounds of the traffic in Commercial Road died away and Silent Street resembled its name. There was the long wall of a warehouse and yard on one side and a row of low houses on the other. The skylights in the warehouse were boarded over, and odd slates were broken in the roofs of the houses, but otherwise Ginger couldn't see much damage. But he couldn't see far. All the streets were hemmed in so.

His pace quickened as he reached the end of the road. He crossed over at the top and under the railway arch. As he approached Angel Street he heard a goods train shuffling along the embankment. He was almost running when he got to the corner. He turned into the street, and stopped. The dark thoughts he'd been fighting all the way suddenly became realities.

Miss Pilgrim's house had gone.

Vaguely, he saw the rest of it — the railway embankment, the arches at the end, the torn roofs with the make-shift tarpaulins spread over them, the pitted walls and the shored-up end of the house next door. A crumbling wall was all that remained of Miss Pilgrim's house.

Ginger stood there, staring across the street. The rubble had been tidied up. The paving-stones in front of where the little hedge had grown had been re-laid, the cobbles of the road swept clean. The rescue squad and the salvage gang had done their jobs. The place was a dead heap of brick and mortar.

Ginger slowly crossed the road. There was nothing to stop him walking into the front garden as far as the crater. The boundary wall at the back was still standing. It marked the end of the garden. The garden seemed very small, but when he'd first seen it as a boy he'd thought it enormous. Now you couldn't see the patch of grass for the brick dust; but there was a pink flower coming through near the wall. Ginger thought it was an aster. Right at the end in the corner where the joint of the wall was split, he could see a little heap of wood with wire netting twisted round it. It looked like a bit of Mr Timothy's run, the one Mr Eccles made.

Ginger heard the footsteps on the pavement but he didn't look round until they stopped.

"Mornin', mate," the man said. He was in the uniform of a warden. He had a friendly face with a snub nose, and a steel helmet strapped over his right shoulder. He looked very tired. He stared at Ginger with dull, sympathetic eyes. "Didya know the lady what lived 'ere?"

"Yes," said Ginger. He didn't want to talk about it but he had to know. "Was she alone?"

"She lived alone," the warden said.

"Yes," Ginger said again. "With a cat."

"Dunno nothin's abaht a cat," the warden said. "But a rel'tive was over 'ere soon arter it 'appened. Nice gal she was. Nurse or sumthin'. Took it very well, she did, considerin' it was so soon arter-like."

"Where is she now?" Ginger asked.

"I dunno. Gorn back ter the 'orspital, I s'ppose."

Ginger came out on to the pavement.

"When did it happen?" he asked.

The warden rubbed his nose with a grimy hand.

"It's 'appenin' all the time, mate," he said. "But this lot copped it abaht a week ago. Dunno fer cert'n. I warn't on dooty 'ere that night. But they c'n tell yer fer sure back at the post." He suddenly peered into Ginger's face. "Blimey, mate, ya lorst yer colour. D'ya feel all right?"

"Yes," said Ginger quietly. He felt sick and hollow inside. He was thinking about the grand reunion.

The warden took him gently by the arm. A cheerful glint had come into his eye.

"What ya need, cock, is a good strong cup o' char. Better come back ter the post. 'Arry there, 'e's the tea-boy. Makes the best cup o' char this side o' Aldgate Pump."

They began to walk up the street, but Ginger stopped.

"I must find Jo," he said.

"Eh? Who must yer find, mate?"

"The girl you saw. The relative," Ginger said. "She works at the hospital in Hertfordshire, but I don't know where."

The warden's frown lifted.

"Soon put that right for yer, mate." His voice was cocky, buoyant. "Bound ter 'ave 'er address at the post. We never slips hup over fhings like that. Come on now."

They started walking again. The warden glanced at Ginger out of the corner of his eye. He didn't know the lad. Indeed, he didn't know many of the folk in the district. He came from Bow.

"Yer warn't a rel'tive, I don't s'ppose?" he asked at length.

"No," said Ginger quietly. "Just a friend."

They turned right by the railway arches, walked a little way down Colman Row, then turned left. Ginger hardly noticed their surroundings. The shrapnel-pitted roofs and walls, the boarded windows, the acrid atmosphere of smoke and decay and destruction. He hardly noticed, until they got to the railway bridge. Then he stopped, staring at the empty gateway to Mr Eccles's joinery yard. What remained of the gates sagged on their hinges. Inside was a mess of blackened timbers. The walls of the shop were a mound of ash; burnt rafters lay across the charred benches; the little paint store, the ladders and all the scaffolding had gone.

The warden saw Ginger staring.

"Incend'ries," he said.

"I used to work there," said Ginger, still staring. "Is Mr Eccles all right?"

"One o' the lucky 'uns," the warden said enviously. "'E jus' sold the outfit in time. Not a month since."

Ginger was surprised and relieved.

"Yus, 'e was lucky all right," went on the warden. "I saw 'im 'ere the day 'e sold it. 'Ad ter sell, 'e did, on account o' 'is missus. Bit o' nerve trouble, it was. Doctor said she'd gotta get out. They was livin' at Man'r Park. So 'e ups and sells the bus'ness and 'is 'ouse an' all, an' goes orf ter the country. Got 'is eye on a li'le place, 'e 'ad. Small'oldin', 'e said it was."

They moved on under the railway bridge and over the canal towards the warden's post.

"That's what he always wanted," Ginger said.

CHAPTER
ELEVEN

The bus from St Albans dropped Ginger at the top of the lane. He could see the hospital gates at the end of it. Tall, wrought-iron, they were. It looked like the entrance to a great country house. When he reached the gravel drive and saw the rambling building in the distance he knew it was a great country house, turned into a hospital.

It was a lovely afternoon. The sun was low in the sky, but the air was warm and scented. The branches of the elms threw a filigree pattern of shadow across the drive. The chorus of birds surrounded him. Cheeky sparrows hopped among the shrubs on either side. Somewhere a church clock struck five. The war seemed a long way away. Only the hospital, through the trees, brought it close to you.

Some of the parkland was under the plough. He could see a golden patch of stubble where the corn had been cut. But along the drive and round the big house and outbuildings the grass grew rich and green and there were trees and rhododendron shrubs. On one side the grassland sloped gently away from him. He could see a small lichen-covered cottage, with a stream close by. The water shimmered in the sunshine, throwing up a halo of dazzling light that gave a dream-like appearance to the cows grazing the pasture on the other side. Ginger suddenly thought of Mr Eccles. Mr Eccles had got his acre or two. Ginger wondered about the Jersey cow and the greenhouse and the stream to fish in. Perhaps a dream like this one. Funny how it took a war to make a dream come true. War was a killer of dreams.

Ginger heard the voices before he saw the little group on the hospital steps. One moment there'd been no one; now he could see three people outside the main doors. A man and two girls. They wore long white coats and looked very official.

The man suddenly turned and went into the hospital. The two girls came down the steps. One of them went along the path towards the outbuildings. Ginger didn't know what the other was going to do until she happened to look in his direction. Then she stood motionless, staring. A slim figure with fluffy dark hair. Ginger was sure she had dimples, and he knew before she started running towards him, it was Jo.

She threw her arms around him. He could feel her breath on his cheek.

"Ginger! Oh — Ginger! How wonderful to see you." Her eyes were all over him; but he didn't know where to look. He was trembling, shy, embarrassed by Jo's ardent welcome. He thought all the hospital would see; but there was only a sparrow looking.

Ginger had primed himself. He knew what he was going

to say, what he was going to do; but now the moment had come he was tongue-tied. Could do nothing.

Jo stepped back, holding his hands, looking at him.

"I hardly knew you in your uniform," she said. "And a corporal, too."

"Lance-corporal," Ginger said quietly. It seemed a silly thing to say at such a moment, but it was better than nothing at all.

"I was getting worried about you," Jo said gravely. "I hadn't heard and you didn't come. Didn't you get my letter or the wire?"

"I've had nothing." Ginger frowned.

Jo's wide eyes opened wider. Her lower lip trembled.

"So you haven't heard — about Aunt Ann —?"

"Yes." Ginger swallowed. "I've been to Angel Street. I heard everything at the air raid post. That's where I got your address."

"Oh, Ginger, what an awful muddle." Jo looked away. "I wrote you a letter last week, and after — after it happened, I sent a wire. I didn't say anything. Just asking you to get in touch." She turned her face to him. "I didn't want to make it worse for you, Ginger. There was nothing you or anyone could do. We know we did all we could. Aunt Ann was so self-willed. I was afraid it would come."

Ginger bowed his head.

"They didn't even find Mr Timothy," he said at length.

Jo's eyes were soft, but there were no more tears behind them.

"No," she said. "He wouldn't have wanted to live without her."

They stood for a minute quite still and silent. Then Jo suddenly put her arm through Ginger's.

"I'm not very polite," she said. "Keeping you standing out here after you've come all this way."

Ginger liked the feel of her arm through his.

"I've only come up from Ternfield," he said. They set off across the grass towards the lichen-covered cottage. "I'm stationed there now. Posted down from Scotland last week. If you sent the letter and wire up there, I expect they're still following me."

"I did. To Scotland." Jo brushed a curl from her eye. "I didn't know when you were leaving or where you were going."

"I wrote to Angel Street just before I left," Ginger explained. "I reckon you can guess how I felt, not hearing anything."

Jo squeezed his arm. She didn't say anything. Neither of them spoke again until they were close to the cottage. Then Ginger stopped suddenly.

He said: "Where're we going? I've been so confused I can't think straight. Where're you taking me?"

"Home to tea, of course. I've just come off duty, and you've a hungry look." She gave him an anxious glance. "Don't say your leave is up already?"

"No fear — no — I — but d'you live here then?" Ginger's eyes raked over the place in awe.

"Me and three other girls." Jo smiled faintly. "It used to be the fishing lodge. The hospital authorities have made a lot of alterations since they took over the estate." She led him to the door. "They've made this into a couple of flatlets, sort of. I share the upstairs with another radiographer. And there're two below. We've got a communal bath in the outhouse, there." Jo pointed a slim finger at the lean-to addition, and led the way upstairs.

They went through a tiny kitchen into the plainly furnished living-room. It all looked very cosy under the low ceiling beams with chintz curtains framing the lattice windows. Jo invited Ginger to sit down and make himself at home, but the only way he could make himself at home was to help her lay the tea. So she got him to take in the crockery and cut the bread and butter.

When the table was set Jo crossed to the door at the other end of the room. She had a strange gleam in her eye.

"You haven't seen everything yet," she said. "This is the bedroom." She opened the door.

Ginger wondered why Jo had suddenly remembered the bedroom when they were about to have tea. But he left the chair he was going to sit on and went towards her. Half-way across the sound stopped him. It was a faint, plaintive sound. It sent a queer, familiar feeling through him. His gaze fell to Jo's feet. He couldn't believe his eyes. There was a kitten there. That was surprising enough, but the surprising thing of all, the thing that took his breath away, was its appearance. It looked exactly like Mr Timothy. In miniature, of course, but exactly, all the same. The white chin and bib, the little spats on each paw, the rest all silky black. It fussed around Jo's feet, tail up straight, eyes wide, mouth open.

"Gosh, Jo." Ginger's voice trembled. He bent down and took the little creature tenderly in his hands. "Where did he come from?"

Jo shut the bedroom door and came close.

"Angel Street," she said softly.

Ginger stared at her, his finger stroking the kitten's chin. The kitten wrapped his front paws round the middle joint.

"But he's the image of — Mr Timothy," Ginger said.

"Yes," said Jo. "Anyone can see he's Mr Timothy's son. I knew he'd be a lovely surprise for you."

The kitten put his tongue out. He looked as though he was laughing. Ginger was lost for words.

"I found him in the rubble," Jo said.

"But they never said anything about a kitten at the warden's post."

"I don't suppose they knew. And they've other things to think about." Jo looked thoughtful, a little sad. "I went back to Angel Street when I left the warden's post. I don't know why. I just had to see the place again. It was a funny sort of feeling I had. Everyone had gone. I climbed over the rubble into the back garden. And that's when I heard the cry. I found him in a hole under some bricks near where the garden wall had split. Behind what was left of Mr Timothy's run." Jo stroked the kitten's head. "It was a miracle he was still alive."

"Yes," said Ginger. "It's a miracle all right. But how could Mr Timothy be his father? Mr Timothy never went out."

"He must have got out when Aunt Ann was ill," Jo said. "The woman who came in and looked after her must have let him go."

Ginger still had doubts.

"But even if he did get out," he said. "How come the kitten to be there, in Miss Pilgrim's garden?" He hesitated, shy. "I mean, a mother cat would have kept her kitten at home. Not taken him to a stranger's place."

"You know what I think?" Jo suddenly looked like a little girl with secrets.

"What?" said Ginger.

"I think Mr Timothy was a she," Jo said.

They sat down at the table. Jo with the kitten on her lap. She poured some milk into a saucer. The kitten began to purr. He raised himself, his front paws on the table, and started to lap the milk. The milk splashed over his nose and wetted his whiskers. Ginger thought they were the longest whiskers of any kitten he'd ever seen.

"I shall have to make him a stool," he said. "He should have his own place at the table."

"And a birthday, too," said Jo.

"We must start him right, from the beginning. Teach him his manners. It'll take time." He looked at the kitten. Jo was looking at Ginger, and there was that look in her eyes that every woman knows.

"We'll have plenty of time, Ginger," she said.

The kitten didn't understand. He was only interested in the milk. He licked the saucer clean, and Jo put him on the chair between them. He began to wash himself.

Ginger sat silent, watching him wash, just like Miss Pilgrim had done all that time ago. It seemed a long way to Angel Street. A long way back to Sunday teas; a November afternoon, a broken barrow, a little girl with a frightened cat. It was a long way back, though it really hadn't taken long to complete the circle. But it was still a mystery. A miracle and a mystery no one could explain. Was this little orphan really Mr Timothy's son? Was Mr Timothy a Mister even? Who could say?

Only Miss Pilgrim and Mr Timothy knew.